Pregnant!

Joelle supposed that she should have considered the possibility that she had been pregnant all along. She'd had her suspicions, but she hadn't wanted to believe them. But now she had no choice. She was four weeks pregnant with Gabriel Lafleur's child.

She considered calling Gabriel, and then tossed the idea aside. What good would it do? She knew for a fact that he didn't want a wife any more than she wanted a husband. She had absolutely no reason in the world to think that Gabriel Lafleur wanted to hear from her.

Still, several nights later, Joelle found herself dialing his telephone number. Of course, she had no intention of telling him about the baby. She simply wanted to hear his voice, make small talk for a while and then hang up.

His telephone rang once...twice...three times.

"Hello...?"

Dear Reader,

This month Silhouette Romance has six irresistible novels for you, starting with our FABULOUS FATHERS selection, *Mad for the Dad* by Terry Essig. When a sexy single man becomes an instant dad to a toddler, the independent divorcée next door offers parenthood lessons—only to dream of marriage and motherhood all over again!

In *Having Gabriel's Baby* by Kristin Morgan, our BUNDLES OF JOY book, a fleeting night of passion with a handsome, brooding rancher leaves Joelle in the family way—and the dad-to-be insisting on a marriage of convenience for the sake of the baby....

Years ago Julie had been too young for the dashing man of her dreams. Now he's back in town, and Julie's still hoping he'll make her his bride in *New Year's Wife* by Linda Varner, part of her miniseries HOME FOR THE HOLIDAYS.

What's a man to do when he has no interest in marriage but is having trouble resisting the lovely, warm and wonderful woman in his life? Get those cold feet to the nearest wedding chapel in *Family Addition* by Rebecca Daniels.

In *About That Kiss* by Jayne Addison, Joy Mackey, sister of the bride, is sure her sis's ex-fiancé has returned to sabotage the wedding. But his intention is to walk down the aisle with Joy!

And finally, when a woman shows up on a bachelor doctor's doorstep with a baby that looks just like him, everyone in town mistakenly thinks the tiny tot is his in Christine Scott's *Groom on the Loose*.

Enjoy!

Melissa Senate, Senior Editor

Please address questions and book requests to:
Silhouette Reader Service
U.S.: 3010 Walden Ave., P.O. Box 1325, Buffalo, NY 14269
Canadian: P.O. Box 609, Fort Erie, Ont. L2A 5X3

HAVING GABRIEL'S BABY

Kristin Morgan

Silhouette

R O M A N C E™

Published by Silhouette Books

America's Publisher of Contemporary Romance

SILHOUETTE BOOKS

ISBN 0-373-19199-5

HAVING GABRIEL'S BABY

Copyright © 1997 by Barbara Lantier Veillon

This edition published by arrangement with Harlequin Books S.A.

® and TM are trademarks of Harlequin Books S.A., used under license.
Trademarks indicated with ® are registered in the United States Patent
and Trademark Office, the Canadian Trade Marks Office and in other
countries.

Printed in U.S.A.

KRISTIN MORGAN

lives in Lafayette, Louisiana, the best heart of Acadiana, where the French language of her ancestors is still spoken fluently by her parents and grandparents. Happily married to her high school sweetheart, she has three children. She and her husband have traveled all over the South, as well as other areas of the United States and Mexico, and they both count themselves lucky that their favorite city, New Orleans, is only two hours away from Lafayette.

In addition to her writing, she enjoys cooking and preparing authentic Cajun food for her family with recipes passed on to her through generations. Her hobbies include reading—of course!—flower gardening and fishing. She loves walking in the rain, newborn babies, all kinds of music, chocolate desserts and love stories with happy endings. A true romantic at heart, she believes all things are possible with love.

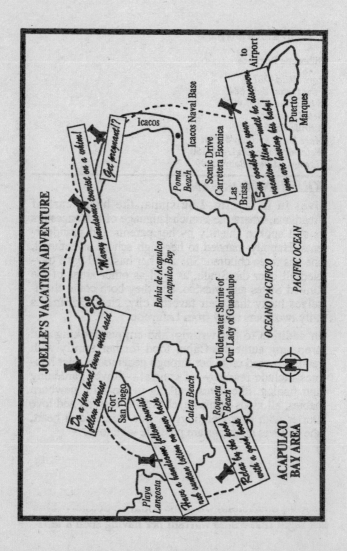

JOELLE'S VACATION ADVENTURE

Warn handsome tourist on a cabin!

Get pregnant!?

Icacos

Icacos Naval Base

Scenic Drive
Carretera Esenica

Poma
Beach

Las
Brisas

to
Airport

Say goodbye to your
vacation fling until he discovers it's
you are having his baby!

Puerto
Marques

Do a few local bars with said fellow tourist

Bahia de Acapulco
Acapulco Bay

PACIFIC OCEAN

OCEANO PACIFICO

PACIFIC OCEAN

Fort
San Diego

There a handsome fellow tourist
rub suntan lotion on your back

Caleta Beach

Roqueta
Beach

Underwater Shrine of
Our Lady of Guadalupe

Relax by the pool
with a good book

Playa
Langosta

ACAPULCO
BAY AREA

be thirsty this morning. After all, she had a sound nine hours of sleep...

Chapter One

As the bright morning sunlight poured in through the two-inch opening in the drapes of her hotel room window, Joelle Ames turned over in bed and groaned when a sharp, excruciating pain shot across her forehead from temple to temple.

What she wouldn't have given in that moment for a couple of aspirin. In fact, after moving her head again, ever so slightly, she quickly decided that maybe she needed three of the painkillers, instead. Not to mention, a cold ice pack placed right at a certain spot on her forehead.

Obviously this, her last day of vacation in Acapulco, wasn't going to be one of her better days. She had come here from her hometown of San Diego five days ago for a badly-needed rest and, since her arrival, had purposefully kept a low profile. In fact, she couldn't understand what she could've possibly done last night that would warrant her having such a terrible headache first thing this morning. After all, since it was her last night of vacation, she'd simply gone to dinner with Gabriel Lafleur, the farmer from Louisiana who had somehow become her touring partner over the past few days. Sure, he was one sexy-looking man, and she had let herself relax for the first time in—What?—Years?—and enjoy his company. But that's all it was. One night of fun. Now it was over with. She just wished her headache was, too.

If only she could've found the courage to pry open her eyelids, climb out of bed and walk over to where her luggage was to see if she had brought along any painkillers with her.

If only she could collect her thoughts.

But the truth of the matter was, it hurt too much for her to try to think straight right now. In fact, losing consciousness would've been a blessing at this point. Unfortunately, though, it was obvious that she wasn't going to be given that luxury.

Suddenly a brief flash of memory from her actions last night crossed Joelle's mind and she recalled herself dancing in a little, quaint, out-of-the-way cantina. And there was laughter. Lots and lots of laughter. And she and Gabriel Lafleur having a couple of shots of tequila at the crowded bar. *At least, a couple.* My goodness, she'd never drunk that much before in her life. Hadn't the plan been to stop in for just one nightcap? Then what in the world had gotten into her to make her get so sidetracked?

Actually her recollection of last night was shaky, at best. It was as though the bitter pain in her head was deliberately blocking out her memory. What, she wondered, had she done between the time she and Gabriel had left the cantina and now? Maybe if she rang Gabriel's room, which was two floors above her, he could fill in the missing pieces.

She groaned, again, this time after turning over and lying flat on her back. She'd never hurt this bad in her life. A second later she realized that she was completely naked under the sheet covering her—and an immediate alarm went off in her head. Uh-oh. She never slept nude. And she never drank too much, either. Something definitely wasn't right.

Headache, or not, Joelle decided that it was time she faced the world and made sense of her surroundings. Rubbing her eyelids with the tips of her fingers, she finally found the will to force them open and stare at the ceiling in her hotel room. After a moment, she darted her eyes around the room. Exactly what she expected to find, she wasn't sure. Then, just as her gaze fell upon a pair of men's pants tossed across the back of a chair near her bed, the door to her bathroom swung open, and none other than Gabriel Lafleur, her dinner date from last night, stepped through it. His dark brown hair was wet and tousled, and he was naked except for the white towel that was wrapped around his waist. Joelle's stomach did a flat-out belly-bust dive for the floor.

As he strolled forward, his eyes lifted and met hers. Halting as though a steel wall had suddenly dropped down in front of him, he paused a moment before saying in a deep voice, "Well, good morning. I see you've finally awakened."

Shocked speechless—not to mention, mindless—Joelle could only gape at him as her stomach tightened into knots. For a brief moment she thought the sudden wave of heat that swarmed over her and made her sick to her stomach would send her running right past him for the bathroom. As it was, the entire room seemed to fade momentarily before her eyes. She heard her own raspy intake of breath.

"Hey, come on, now. You're not going to pass out on me, are you?" she heard him saying. It was enough to make her inhale deeply and, somehow, the room came back into focus.

By this time Gabriel Lafleur had already walked up to the foot of her bed and was now frowning down as if he halfway expected her to fall apart at the seams. She knew that look well. Her father always used it when he wanted to let her know that she'd somehow failed him, again. And, of course, according to her father, she was always failing him. In fact, if her father had had his wish when she was born thirty-one years ago, he would've been given a son to follow in his footsteps, not a daughter who seemed to falter every time she tried.

Joelle's glare wavered momentarily. She felt vulnerable...*naked*...and mortified to the bone to have this man she hardly knew staring down at her and probably making snap judgments of her character— or, rather, her lack of it. Certainly he had no right to do that. After all, he hardly knew anything at all about her, other than the fact that she'd obviously made a huge mistake last night in thinking that he was a decent enough guy to have dinner with. Nonetheless, if he thought she was going to fall to pieces right there in front of him as if she was some weak little woman with no backbone, he was in for a big disappointment. She no longer gave her father the benefit of seeing her tears. Therefore, humiliated, or not, she wasn't about to let this man see them, either. Instead she conjured up her best poker face and glared at him.

But, regardless of what she hoped was an Oscar winning performance on her part, the following moments grew increasingly difficult for Joelle. She stared in surprised defiance at Gabriel Lafleur...at his bare, lean, muscled chest, and at the way the dark curly hair at its center lay damp and matted against his tanned skin. Finally, having a will of their own, her eyes began following a drop of water as it slid downward, only to have it eventually soaked up by the hotel guest towel wrapped tightly around his slim waistline. Her throat felt suddenly dry...parched, and swallowing in that moment became difficult. Her eyes lifted to his and what she saw there made her realize that he was aware of her every thought. Finally, unable to deal with this reality for a second longer, she squeezed her eyes shut and prayed that when she opened them, again, he would be gone.

Obviously her father had been right about her all along. Obviously there was a part of her that was too soft...too womanly, to hold up under the pressure of a man's world. Surely, if she had any strength of character at all, she wouldn't be in such a humiliating situation.

Joelle knew her prayers weren't going to be answered when she felt him touch her arm and say, "Hey, are you going to be all right?" The feel of his warm fingers on her flesh startled her. Her eyes sprang wide open, and they stared at each other as if they were two cat burglars who were suddenly surprised to discover themselves on the same rooftop.

Eventually Joelle found her voice. "Of course, I'm going to be all right," she snapped.

"Thank goodness for that," he replied. "About all I need this morning is to find myself at the mercy of a woman in tears."

"What are you doing in my room?" Joelle demanded, although, in truth, she feared she already knew the answer to that one. She was just hoping like everything that her gut instincts were wrong. But, one thing she knew for sure. He wasn't going to find this woman in tears.

"Well…" Gabriel Lafleur said, now grinning down at her with white, even teeth and the most clear brown eyes she'd ever seen. He had wide, full lips that, even in the stark brightness of morning reality, beckoned to be kissed. He had high prominent cheekbones and a squared-off jawline, and a nose that flared slightly wider at the end. In essence, he was six feet of pure, unadulterated male. "I was…uh…just making myself at home," he said, politely. He acted as though being in her hotel room was seemingly of no consequence to him. At least, not like it was to her. "Look, I hope you don't mind that I used your shower," he continued. "But under the circumstances, I didn't think that you would."

Joelle swallowed. "Uh… And what circumstances might that be?" she asked hesitantly, her eyes flicking back up to his handsome face after lingering far too long on a lower, more private part of his anatomy. Thank goodness he still had that towel on. As much as some wanton part of her liked looking at every follicle inch of him, she wished that she could've just snapped her fingers and have him disappear from her hotel room.

His grin widened. "Don't you remember?"

Joelle blinked. Twice. "Remember what?"

"What we did?"

Joelle's heart hammered against her breastbone. "What did we do?"

His eyes narrowed. "You don't remember, do you?"

Joelle gripped the ends of the sheet covering her breasts and pulled it up to the base of her throat. "O-of course, I do. W-we had dinner together."

"And..."

"And...uh...we stopped in at some lively little cantina for a nightcap." Joelle felt quite pleased with herself for having been able to recall that much. At least he wasn't going to think her a complete idiot.

"And then..." he said.

She stared at him blankly.

He stared back. A moment later he said, "See, it's like I thought. You don't remember, do you?"

Hesitating with her answer, Joelle continued to hold the ends of the sheet in a death grip while trying to force her memory from last night to come forward. But the only result was some additional pounding in her already throbbing head. "No, I don't."

"Well, don't feel so bad. 'Cause I don't, either."

Her eyes widened. "What do you mean?"

"Well...I mean, I think it's pretty obvious that we came back here and spent the night together." He paused then, long enough to give the impression that he was waiting on her to make a comment.

But Joelle had no comment at this point. As it was, having her mistake said out loud made her feel sick to her stomach, all over again.

Staring down at her, Gabriel Lafleur used his fingers to comb back his damp hair from his forehead. "Look, to be perfectly frank with you," he continued, "my memory of what we did from the time we left the cantina until I awakened this morning in your bed is a bit hazy. I can only assume that neither of us recognized the numbing effect of the tequila we were drinking, and it just slipped up on us."

"In other words, you're saying we both got drunk."

"Yeah," he said with a slow shake of his head. "That pretty much sums it up."

Once again, Joelle squeezed her eyes closed. "Oh, God, how could I have done something so foolish?"

"Look," Gabriel said, "I just need to know one thing."

Opening her eyes, Joelle exhaled deeply. "Like I just said, Lafleur, I don't remember anything. And, quite frankly, I'd prefer to leave it that way."

His gaze was challenging. "Yeah, well, that's fine with me, Ames, except for one thing."

Once more, Joelle exhaled deeply. Leave it to a man, she thought, to want to recall every nitty-gritty detail of their night spent in bed together. "What's that?"

"Did we get married first?"

Clutching the sheet against her breasts, Joelle sat straight up in bed. "What?"

He looked her square in the face. "Did we get married last night before coming back to the hotel?"

"Are you crazy? Why on earth would we have done something like that?"

Gabriel Lafleur scratched the side of his head. "Hell if I know. But we're both wearing dime-store wedding rings this morning. I don't know about you, but I wasn't wearing one yesterday." Stunned, Joelle stared at him in awe as he suddenly tried to pull something from around his finger, but he seemed to be having a bit of difficulty getting it over his knuckle. "And," he said, as he continued his efforts, "if I remember correctly, at some point last night you said that you wouldn't sleep with a guy unless you were ready to have some kind of a permanent commitment with him."

Dazed, Joelle lifted her left hand in midair and gazed at her ring finger as if it was a lighted firecracker ready to explode. But a moment later, she regained her equilibrium and simply slipped off the cheap-looking ring that she knew was sold by any street vendor in any vacation hot spot in the world. She placed it on the bedside table next to her as if it was no big deal. Which it wasn't, of course. Still, her heart raced ahead like mad. As if she had just discovered herself running in a marathon and knew her life depended on her winning it.

Taking a deep, steadying breath, Joelle looked back at him and tilted her chin a fraction higher. "Yeah— well, I can tell you right now, if you had the nerve last night to suggest that we sleep together, you can bet I said something like that to you. Look, I know what you must be thinking of me right now, but the truth is, I don't happen to get drunk with men I hardly know. Nor do I sleep around."

"Hey, you don't have to prove anything to me," he said. "But, regardless of what you say, it doesn't change the fact that I remember us leaving the cantina together last night with the dumb idea in mind of finding someone to marry us. Hell, I just want to know if we succeeded."

Squeezing her eyes shut, Joelle grimaced. She, too, now vaguely recalled having done something of similar nature last night. But in the cold light of day, it was simply too farfetched an idea for her to actually believe it possible. Her memory was undoubtedly playing tricks on her. Or…or, maybe, Gabriel Lafleur had somehow set her up to make her believe what he wanted.

With renewed determination, she opened her eyes and glared at him.

"That's ridiculous. I would never do such an inconceivable thing," Joelle replied, stubbornly, but—in spite of her efforts to convince herself otherwise—her heart was beginning to palpitate uncontrollably, because somewhere deep, down inside, the memory was growing stronger. "You're making that part up."

"'Fraid not."

Her eyes widened. "Are you trying to tell me that we might've gotten married last night for the sole purpose of sleeping together?"

"'Fraid so. Or—so it would seem."

"No way."

"Lady, if I remember correctly, you were the one setting up the rules, not me."

"Hey, now, look here. I can assure you, I didn't coerce you into anything," Joelle stammered.

"Well, neither did I," he replied.

"I certainly didn't come to Acapulco to find a husband."

Gabriel's hands went to his hips. "Well, I certainly didn't come here to find myself a wife, that's for sure, and I don't like having to deal with this any more than you do. I'm only praying that we couldn't find anyone to do the job and ended up just crawling into the sack together. It certainly would make things a whole lot less complicated this morning."

Indeed, it would, Joelle thought. But, in spite of her initial reaction, a moment later she felt a sinking feeling in the pit of her stomach at the distinct thought of her having just crawled into bed with him. She had morals that she lived by, after all. Morals that had been pounded into her head since she was a child by a strict, disciplinarian father. But she didn't owe this man a quick briefing of her character upbringing. Besides, what good would it do at this point?

Therefore, in order to hide her growing anxiety, Joelle continued to glare at him and said, "How can you not remember what we did last night?"

He shrugged. "The same as you, I guess. Too much tequila."

"Oh, God," Joelle said, making sure that the sheet she held against her continued to cover her nakedness as she swung her legs over the edge of the bed and planted her feet on the floor. She hung her pounding head in the palm of one hand. After all that had gone wrong in her life lately, she couldn't believe that this, too, was happening to her. "This is awful," she groaned.

Gabriel Lafleur placed his hands on his hips and sighed heavily. "Yeah—well—believe me, I know exactly what you mean."

Then, in almost the same breath, he said, "Listen up. It seems to me that if we got married last night, then we ought to have some kind of proof—right? I mean, like a marriage certificate—or—or, something." He turned away from her suddenly, stepped up to the dresser where a few of her personal belongings were on the top and began rummaging through them, searching, no doubt, for some kind of proof. Coming up empty-handed, he turned once again and targeted

Joelle with those clear brown eyes of his. "Well, don't just sit there. Get up and help me look, for heaven's sake. You said that you didn't want this to be happening any more than I did."

The frustration in his voice was enough to spark Joelle into action. "I don't," she replied, haughtily. She stood immediately and began searching her hotel room on her own, scanning tabletops...the floor... under the bed. She found her panty and bra, and Gabriel's tie and Jockey shorts. All four items were hiding beneath the quilted bedspread on the floor at the foot of the bed. She found her white poet's blouse and the navy blue straight skirt she'd worn to dinner last night thrown on the seat of the chair where his slacks were. With each piece of clothing she found, it became clear to her that both of them had apparently been more than eager to shed their clothes and climb into bed together—with or without the benefit of marriage—and, as a result, her face grew redder and redder with embarrassment. And right along with her renewed embarrassment came a whole new set of memories from last night. Distinct, clear images of her and Gabriel kissing in the elevator as it had taken them up to her floor. And there was another jarring memory of him carrying her across the threshold. *Like they were married.* And, of course, there was the one of them making love on her bed...

In fact, her memories were now so tantalizingly frank in their recollection of what she and Gabriel had done together, Joelle found herself breaking into a cold sweat as she reached for her shoulder-strap purse that hung on a door knob. She began searching its contents. In truth, she didn't want to recall the sensuous details of having been in his arms any more than she really wanted to find a marriage certificate declaring them as husband and wife. After all, she'd already made one mistake by getting drunk and sleeping with him. Why compound the problem this morning by hoping to find proof of a marriage that neither of them wanted?

"Find anything?" he asked, coming up right behind her. Her stomach bottomed out.

"Uh...not yet," she replied, curtly. She could smell the clean freshness of the soap he'd used while showering. Suddenly feeling the need to place added distance between them, she stepped to one side and turned. "How about you?"

"Not yet," he replied. Joelle noticed that his eyes dropped momentarily to where her hands held the sheet over her breasts and, once again, her stomach quivered.

Joelle gave him a scathing look. Considering that he was wrapped in only a towel, he really had some nerve to look at her as if she was the only one undressed.

Clearing his throat, he ran his fingers through his hair. "That's probably a good thing. Look, maybe it means that we decided not to get married, after all. Or, maybe we just gave up on the idea because we couldn't find anyone qualified to perform the ceremony."

"Maybe," Joelle grumbled. "But, unfortunately, I don't think my luck these days is running that high. Considering our inebriated state, we could've gotten married and then simply lost the document on our way back here."

Gabriel frowned, and Joelle could tell from the expression on his face that her theory wasn't at all to his liking. Well, it certainly wasn't to hers, either.

Still, she wasn't quite ready to give up all hope of finding a simple resolution that would allow them to part company without worry or fanfare. Surely one of them would find something to jar their memory and, hopefully, give them both some badly needed peace of mind. With that in mind, Joelle proceeded to check the zipper compartments of her purse, but she found nothing. "Did you look through all your pockets?" she asked.

"I checked my pants. I haven't found my shirt, yet."

"Here it is," Joelle stated, using her middle finger to pick up his wrinkled white dress shirt off the floor by its collar. She turned in his direction and offered it to him. As he reached for it, his eyes met hers, and he smiled.

"Thanks."

"You're welcome."

"Look, Joelle, about last night . . ."

"Forget it. It was as much my fault as it was yours."

"Yeah . . . well, that's not exactly what I was going to say."

"Oh."

"Look, I . . . uh . . . about the sex . . . I mean, it was great you know."

Joelle thought her insides would turn inside-out. Yes, she knew, but she didn't want to know. "Uh, look, I don't really remember any of it, okay?" *Liar.* "And I'd like to keep it that way."

"Hey, whatever you say," he replied, shrugging lightly.

Joelle glanced up and their gazes locked. Within moments, though, she realized her mistake in thinking she could handle such a battle of wills with him and she shook herself. What, in heaven's name, she wondered, did she think she was doing, gazing up at him that way? Here the two of them were, alone and practically strangers, with one of them wrapped in a bath towel, and the other in a bed sheet. Was she completely crazy, or just a glutton for punishment?

She took several steps away from him. He gave her a haunted look as he reached into his shirt pocket and came out a second later with a white folded piece of paper held tightly between his two fingers. Joelle's heart skipped a beat. "What's that?" she asked, breathlessly. She was at his side in a flash.

"I don't know," he said, releasing an anxious breath. He started to carefully unfold the piece of paper, only to discover that it was just a regular sheet of white, lined, loose-leaf paper. But written on it in a sprawling, amateurish handwriting were yesterday's date and the words: *Gabriel and Joelle, I now pronounce you man and wife. Signed, José Cuervo.*

José Cuervo was the brand name of the tequila they had drunk last night.

Dazed for several moments, neither of them spoke. Finally, Joelle couldn't take the deafening silence another moment. "What does that paper mean?" she asked in a whispered voice. It was as though if she spoke too loudly, the entire world would know her most recent sin.

Still staring down at the piece of paper in his hands, Gabriel Lafleur didn't answer her. Finally she nudged him in the ribs with her elbow. "Lafleur, I need you to answer me. What does the note mean?"

"Hell, if I know," he grumbled, suddenly crumpling up the piece of paper in one hand and tossing it like a basketball toward a nearby trash can. It fell inside like a dead ringer, and he said, "Bingo. See, now we're off the hook. It's in the trash."

"Are you sure?" Joelle asked, still somewhat stunned from just awakening and finding Gabriel Lafleur in her hotel room, much less the rest of it. She sat down on the edge of the bed in the hopes of giving herself a moment to pull herself back together.

"Look," he said, turning toward her and placing his hands on his hips. Joelle found herself following his every move. He had such wide, sensuous-looking hands.

Those hands had made love to her body last night. Over and over, again.

She was breathless at the thought of it.

Swallowing hard, Joelle flicked her eyes back up to his. "What were you saying?" she asked.

"I was saying, surely you saw for yourself that piece of paper wasn't anything legal. No minister or government official would've given us a handwritten note like that."

"I know that. So, what's your point, Lafleur?" Joelle stated.

"My point is, that piece of paper doesn't prove anything. Certainly it doesn't prove that we're married."

"I understand perfectly. But who could've written it?"

"I haven't the slightest idea," he replied. "Any person on the street, for all I know."

"Then, it wasn't you."

"Me," he said, sounding surprised. "No, of course not."

Then he narrowed his eyes. "Was it you?"

"Dream on," she replied, and for the first time since awakening that morning, she actually considered laughing.

"Well, was it?" he asked, skeptically, and suddenly Joelle realized that the man was actually serious.

"No," she answered.

"Well, in that case, we're back to square one. We still don't know what we did last night."

Suddenly, recalling something very critical in her plans for that day, Joelle gasped. "Oh, my God! What time is it?"

Gabriel glanced over to where his wristwatch lay on a bedside table. "Almost eleven-thirty."

"Oh—my goodness. How could I be so dense? I must be losing it. My flight back home to San Diego leaves in less than an hour—and I'm not even dressed, yet."

She raced to where her luggage sat, all packed up and ready to go—thank goodness—and picked up the outfit folded on top that she planned to wear today. "Do me a favor," she said. "Call a cab and have them waiting for me at the entrance to the hotel in ten minutes." Within seconds of saying that, she was closing the bathroom door behind her.

Minutes later she emerged, showered, dressed and ready to go. At first she thought that Gabriel Lafleur had skipped out on her and the whole messy ordeal— which she quickly decided would've probably been the best way to end this nightmare. But, unfortunately, though the weakening in her knees proved she actually felt otherwise, she saw him a second later, standing at the window with his back to her. He was now wearing the same dark gray pants he'd worn last night.

Without comment, Joelle quickly gathered her personal effects that were still on top of the dresser and dumped them into her cosmetic bag. Then picking up a piece of her luggage in each hand, she cleared her throat in the hopes of getting his attention. *Like he hadn't already heard her rummaging around in the room.* He turned around to face her with his hands in his pockets. "I'm leaving now," she said.

She saw him take in a deep breath. "Look, I don't know what I'm supposed to say at this point."

"Then don't say anything," she replied. Her heart was galloping around in her chest as if it were a wild, caged stallion.

A lopsided, sheepish grin slid up one side of his face. "But I feel like I should say something. I feel like I owe you that much."

"You don't owe me anything, Lafleur. I'm a big girl."

"Somehow I feel that this is all my fault. I'm sorry."

"Look, it just happened, okay? So let's be modern thinking adults about this and just get on with our lives."

"Hey, if you can live with it, then I sure can," he replied. "It's just you seemed to be upset earlier, so I was trying to make you feel better."

Joelle sighed deeply. Truthfully she didn't know if she was ever going to be able to live with herself, again, but, at the moment, she saw that she had no other choice than to try. "Look, for my own peace of mind, once I get back home I plan to have my attorney look into this matter and see if he can come up with anything. If he does, then I'll give him the okay to resolve whatever problem we may have created for ourselves."

Gabriel nodded his head. "That's probably a good idea." He walked to the bedside table where his wristwatch was, picked up a notepad and pencil and jotted something down. "Here," he said a moment later, tearing off a sheet. "This is my telephone number just in case your attorney needs to get in touch with me." He shrugged. "You can never tell."

Joelle hesitated only a second before taking the piece of paper from him and stuffing it inside a pocket of her purse. Then, pulling out one of her business cards, she gave it to him. "Just in case," she said.

"You never know," Gabriel replied.

"True," she said, and for some reason she felt breathless. "I guess we just as soon make this as easy as possible on ourselves."

"I agree."

Joelle turned for the door.

"Hey—Ames," he said in a softer tone of voice. "Wait a minute."

Pivoting around to face him, she lifted her eyebrows in question.

"What do you think? Did we actually get married?"

The question startled her and, for a brief moment, Joelle had no idea how to answer it. But, at the same time, it immediately brought a few things into focus for her. For one thing, she wasn't going to part from this man and have him worry that perhaps she would show up at his doorstep one day, saying they were husband and wife and that he owed her something. He didn't owe her anything.

Gabriel Lafleur didn't know it, of course, but in her everyday life, she was a fully dedicated career woman and was quite capable of taking care of herself under any circumstances. "I—uh—no, I honestly don't think we did."

"Yeah," he said after a moment of hesitation, "that's what I think, too."

"Goodbye, Lafleur," Joelle said. "Have a nice life."

"Goodbye, Ames. Take care."

Then, in spite of a sudden heaviness at the center of her chest, Joelle took a deep, steadying breath, turned and hurried out the door.

She knew it would be the last time she would ever see Gabriel Lafleur again.

And though she hated to admit it, a small part of her regretted it.

It was so silly of her, she knew. Nonetheless, it was true.

Chapter Two

Arriving home that evening, Joelle took a deep, steadying breath, unlocked the door to her high-rise condo and stepped inside. Her telephone was ringing and she thought she knew who it was. If there was anything she could say about her father, it was that he was persistent. Well, she wasn't anywhere near being ready to talk to him just yet. First she needed a couple of aspirin and some sleep, then maybe she'd be ready to confront the world, again. But, for tonight, she had enough on her mind. She stood nearby while allowing her answering machine to pick up the call and listened to see if her initial suspicions were accurate.

And, sure enough, they were. Within a moment she was hearing her father's condescending tone of voice as he demanded that she answer her telephone and talk to him. From the number of messages she saw flashing on her machine, he'd obviously been trying to reach her for days.

Yeah, well, he could try reaching her all he wanted, but she wasn't going to listen to his tirades anymore. Not after the way he'd humiliated her in front of all his employees. After all, it wasn't every day that a daughter, who was always faithful to her father's wishes, found out that he was having another employee within his company spy on her work performance and report those findings back to him. This time she was through allowing him to manipulate her. He might be her father, but he didn't have any right to dictate her life.

This time, though, he'd really hurt her. In fact, he hadn't gone into retirement and turned over his company to her at all. He'd only made her believe that she'd finally won his respect for him to do that, when all the time he was still calling the shots from behind the scenes. Damn him, anyway. He'd made her look like a fool. Well, this was one time she wasn't going to forgive him for it. Nor was she ever going to trust him again to be on her side. But, more importantly, now, more than ever, she was determined to show him that he was wrong about her, and that even without his so-called help, she had the intelligence and tenacity to become highly successful. As much, in fact, as any son of his would have.

She was never going to forgive him.

Never. But, enough of her father for now. At the moment she had other, more urgent things to worry about. Things like Gabriel Lafleur.

No...actually, she really didn't want to think about him, either. The problem was, if only she could stop herself. Wasn't it enough that first thing tomorrow morning she was going to have to contact her attorney and have him look into the matter of her last night in Acapulco? My goodness, couldn't something, somewhere give her a simple break?

It didn't look that way. Because, already images of Gabriel were lurking at the corners of her mind, just waiting to jump forward. One in particular, the one where he was kissing her on the elevator while going up to her room was especially haunting.

It made her stomach quiver.

Her breasts tingle.

It made her feel breathless.

She still wanted him, for heaven's sake. Just as much as she had last night.

How could she recall every little detail of their lovemaking and yet be unable to recall leaving the cantina with him to go get married? And, yet, something in the back of her mind told her that was exactly what she had done. The question was, had they succeeded?

The tension in her neck was so great that she couldn't take it anymore.

Slipping out of her shoes, she turned on the water in her shower and then began unbuttoning her blouse. Moments later she slipped under the warm spray and began shampooing her hair. After stepping out and blowing dry her short shag hairstyle, she dressed in a pale green soft cotton robe. She plodded her way barefoot to the beige sofa in the den, and curled up on one corner with a blanket and pillow and fell sound asleep.

At some point, the doorbell finally woke her, and it became immediately clear that her caller had already grown impatient with her and as a result had his or her finger currently glued to the chime button. Throwing

back the light blanket, Joelle groaned and somehow
got to her feet. Without a doubt, she knew who it was.

Still, as a security measure, she peeked through the
peephole first and then opened the door. The moment she did, her father came barreling across the
threshold as if he were a tyrant on a rampage—which
was normal behavior for him. "Where have you been,
Joelle?" he demanded, his ruddy complexion red-
dened with anger. "I've been calling for days. Didn't
you get any of my messages?"

If there was ever the slightest chance of Joelle getting rid of her headache anytime soon, it had just
quickly skedaddled out of her reach. "I've been out of
town, Father," she said, dryly, dropping back down
on the sofa and laying her pounding head back against
the soft cushion. At any minute, she felt certain that
her head was going to explode into a million pieces.

"That's no excuse," her father declared, standing
over her and glaring down as if he was a mighty eagle
and she, an insignificant little sparrow. His voice
seemed to vibrate through her aching head like the
strumming of a high-pitched guitar. "I was worried
sick about you," he continued as his hands came to
rest on his hips. But, actually, from Joelle's point of
view, his arrogant pose said otherwise.

"I wish I could believe that," she replied, listlessly,
without bothering to lift her head and look at him.
Instead she placed her fingertips against her temples
and began massaging them.

She was still angry at her father. And hurt, too. And
she had every right to be. It was time that Sylvan Ames
realized that she was a real person with feelings and
not just someone put on this earth for him to ridicule
when the mood struck.

"Joelle, have you any idea of how embarrassed I've been by your sudden absence from the marketing firm? Everyone has been asking about you and I've had to lie to them about your whereabouts."

Opening her eyes, Joelle lifted her head and met his stare. "Really? Well, why didn't you just tell them the truth, that I'd resigned on the spot the day I walked out and that I'm no longer an employee of your company?"

"What kind of an idiot do you take me for, Joelle? I'm not about to tell my employees something like that. Now we both know that you just overreacted that day. I'm sure now that you've had time to think about how foolish you looked storming out of the office like that, you're as anxious as I am to put the whole ugly incident behind us and get on with business as usual." Walking briskly toward the door, her father turned just before reaching it. "In fact, be in your office by eight sharp tomorrow morning. We have a new account that needs your attention."

"I'm sorry, Father, but that isn't possible," Joelle replied.

Coming to a sudden halt, her father turned and pinned her to the spot with his glare. "Joelle, I've had about enough of this. I want you to stop behaving like a spoiled child."

"Don't you mean like a silly female?"

"Yes. That, too."

"Well, for your information, Father, I'm not behaving like either. And to prove it, I'm declining your offer of reinstatement. You see, I've decided that it's time that I make it in this world on my own—without your help."

"That's absurd. You'll never do it," Sylvan Ames remarked bitterly.

Joelle sighed. "Yeah—well, neither one of us will ever know that for sure unless I try. And that's what I'm going to do, Father. Surely you can understand my reasons."

Her father narrowed his eyes. "You'll never make it without my help."

"Maybe not. But it's a chance I have to take."

Smirking, her father pointed his finger at her. "You're going to fall flat on your face. But, when you do, don't you dare come crawling back to me. You've had your chance. I'll not be sympathetic to your pleas." Then, pivoting on his heels, he rushed out her door, slamming it behind him.

Hot tears sprang to Joelle's eyes. "You needn't worry, Father. I won't come crawling," she whispered into the extreme silence that immediately followed his departure. "Not for any reason."

Later that night, Joelle opened herself a can of chicken soup for supper. After eating, she went to bed early with an ice pack for her throbbing head. At some point, she began dreaming of Acapulco and Gabriel and woke up the following morning halfway expecting to find her vacation lover asleep in bed beside her. But he wasn't there, and Joelle soon found herself wishing that he was. Eventually she began to realize what she was doing to herself and vowed to put him from her thoughts, once and for all.

But, unfortunately, over the next three weeks Joelle was incapable of pulling herself so completely together that she was able to block out all thoughts of Gabriel. He crept into her mind at the weirdest times, at some of the most inappropriate moments. Sometimes she found him in her thoughts even when she was making plans for her future... plans that, truthfully, here lately, she seemed to have so little energy in trying to accomplish. It wasn't that she was depressed, or sickly, because she wasn't either. The drive was there. It was her get-up-and-go that wasn't.

She was just tired all the time. And sleepy. In fact, no matter how early she went to bed at night, she couldn't seem to get enough sleep. Lately she required an afternoon nap, just to keep going. Finally, after realizing that her condition wasn't improving, she decided that she needed to see a doctor for a good physical and promised to make herself an appointment soon.

But by the time she did, she was quite certain that there was really something seriously wrong with her. She was beginning to wonder if maybe she had picked up some kind of intestinal virus while on vacation.

Gabriel Lafleur stood on the veranda of his large Cajun-styled plantation home, built by his ancestors over a hundred and fifty years ago. It wasn't quite sunup yet, but he knew he should've already been in the cane fields out back. His hired help was already hard at work. But, instead of hurrying to join them, here he was sitting around, sipping on his last cup of coffee and acting like some lovesick fool who had all the time in the world to be thinking about *her.* Hell, it was planting season and he didn't have time to be thinking about anything other than work. Acapulco was weeks ago. It was time he forgot about the woman he'd made love to while there. Heaven help him, it was what he wanted to do more than anything else in the whole world. Only there was a dumb, stubborn part of him that wasn't cooperating with his common sense.

And that's what ate at his gut...constantly... steadily. He didn't even want to think about her. Or, any woman, for that matter. His ex-wife's betrayal had cured him of that. No way would he ever trust another woman enough to make her his wife. Even he wasn't that big a fool.

And, yet, here he was acting just like one. Joelle Ames was, without a doubt, from start to finish, from head to toe, all wrong for him. In fact, that's what made him an even bigger fool than most. He *knew* she was all wrong for him.

He was an idiot. No doubt about it.

Actually, instead of standing around like some lovesick schoolboy, he should've been counting his lucky stars that Joelle Ames was obviously the kind of woman who had been able to put their one-night stand into its proper perspective, just as he had. Some women he knew would've had trouble being that open-minded.

He was surprised that he hadn't heard something— anything—by now from her or her attorney. Under the circumstances, he had felt certain that he would have, if for no other reason than to touch base and clear the air between them one final time. In some ways, maybe he'd been wanting to hear from her.

In fact, one day last week, he'd got to thinking about her—about their night together—and almost picked up the telephone to call. But then he'd decided that maybe it was for the best if he didn't. Certainly he didn't want to stir up any unnecessary trouble for himself. Besides, if she wasn't worrying about any legal problems that might result from their time spent together, then why should he?

Well, in all reality, he did have his family inheritance to worry about. The last thing he needed was for some woman he hardly knew thinking she had some legal claim to it.

But he didn't think that Joelle Ames was that stupid.

Still and all, right now his inheritance wasn't the biggest problem concerning him. *She* was his biggest problem—period.

Damn her, anyway. Why couldn't he simply forget about her?

Suddenly renewing his strong determination to put an end to his thoughts of her—Gabriel set his cup down on the railing that surrounded the porch and headed down the steps toward the fertile fields behind his house. This was the land of his ancestors, the land his father had left him. Located on the western edge of the Atchafalaya Basin in south Louisiana, it was rich, prime soil for toiling sugar cane. But even with all the modern technology and equipment, farming was still a hard way of life. It still took his total commitment, and then some.

But he wasn't complaining. Not really. This was his way of life; it was all he'd ever known, and it was more important to him than anything in the whole world. And it always would be.

Forever.

Therefore, his memories of Ms. Joelle Ames, city-woman personified, could just back off.

Pregnant! Joelle closed the door to her doctor's office as she walked out and stepped into the bright light

of another typical California day. She didn't smile, or
breathe deeply of the crisp, clean breeze as she normally would have. Instead she got into her car and
drove straight home. Once inside, she wandered aim-
lessly from room to room, her nerves too fidgety for
her to think of sitting down for even a moment.

Oh, God, how could something like this be happening to her? She, of all people, who as a dutiful
daughter had never once forgotten her moral upbringing when dealing with the opposite sex. It wasn't
fair that she was going to have to pay such a high price
for her one failure in doing so.

She was suffering from a form of shock, she knew.
Her doctor's unexpected diagnosis for her malaise had
come as a real blow. Actually she supposed that she
should've considered the possibility that she was
pregnant all along. But, the truth of the matter was,
she hadn't. Or, rather, she'd had her suspicions deep,
down inside but she hadn't wanted to believe them.
But now she had no choice. According to her doctor,
she was four weeks pregnant with Gabriel Lafleur's
child.

It was just so difficult for her to believe.

A real life shocker.

She was absolutely terrified.

How could she, of all people, be carrying a child,
when, in fact, she was the last woman on earth meant
for motherhood?

Maybe her doctor had made a mistake.

No—actually, she thought a moment later, the mistake was all her doing. No one had forced her into
sleeping with Gabriel Lafleur. Therefore, it was up to
her to deal with the crisis that had resulted. And,

needless to say, she would do it alone. Without help from anyone. Not even her father.

Especially, not her judgmental father.

Still, Joelle knew her own limitations and was terrified at the prospect of being a single mother. How would she manage to juggle her time between her career and a baby? The fact was, right now, she didn't even have a job. But even if that wasn't a part of the problem, her lack of knowledge about kids and motherhood was. She didn't know an iota about what it took to be a good parent. Her mother had died soon after giving birth to her, and her strict, disciplinarian father had raised her without ever remarrying. Therefore, she'd never had a female role model in her life. Not only that, but her continuous efforts to achieve leadership in a competitive business world had long ago forced her to program out that part of her feminine nature. She had never allowed herself to feel as though she needed a husband and children to be fulfilled as a woman. All she'd ever felt she needed was to have her father's undying respect and had known instinctively that the only way to gain it was by being totally committed to her career.

But now all that was changing.

Now she was going to have a baby.

Dear God, what in the world was she going to do with a baby?

That night, Joelle went to bed and worried herself to sleep. She dreamed of Gabriel and Acapulco and woke up feeling worse than ever.

For the next several days, Joelle thought of little else. But in the end she knew that there was only one option for her and that was to have her baby, and that's all there was to it. Later on, in the coming months, she would deal with what was the best solution for raising her child while still maintaining a full-time career. But for now, her mental plate was overflowing. Though her decision to have her baby had settled her emotions down somewhat, they still weren't anywhere near normal. The truth was, she still had several immediate problems facing her. San Diego was her hometown. She knew lots of people here. Her father was the social climber of the century and worried continuously about his spotless reputation, as if he were an old mother hen. Her pregnancy was going to be an embarrassment for him—and for her, too, no doubt about it. Somehow, she was going to have to find a way to keep her delicate condition a secret from him and everyone else in San Diego, although, deep down inside, she knew that it was going to be virtually impossible. Worse, not only was her father going to be shocked and embarrassed by her pregnancy, but undoubtedly he was going to ridicule her judgment in wanting to keep her baby and she simply couldn't deal with that kind of criticism from him right now.

Which was exactly why, she supposed, that she had automatically tossed aside any thought of telephoning Gabriel Lafleur to tell him about the baby. Like her father, she didn't want him to think that she was needy—clinging—and expecting him to assume responsibility for her problem. After all, she still had her goal of proving to her father—and to the entire world—that she was quite capable of taking care of herself.

Besides, what good would it have done her to call Gabriel? She knew for a fact that he didn't want a wife any more than she wanted a husband. At least, he'd said as much in Mexico, several times, in fact. And according to her attorney, Smith Jamison, thus far, he hadn't been able to find any documented proof that she and Gabriel had gotten married on her last night in Acapulco. She had absolutely no reason in the world to think that Gabriel Lafleur wanted to hear from her, again, under any circumstances. Therefore, it was ridiculous of her to want to call him simply to appease some deep down need in her to hear his voice, again. Absolutely ridiculous.

Still and all, several nights later, in a moment of extreme weakness, when a sudden loneliness swooped down on her and the thought of carrying her child for nine long months without having anyone on her side became unbearable, Joelle found herself dialing his telephone number. Of course, she had no intention of telling him about the baby. She simply wanted to hear his voice, make small talk for a while and then hang up. That would be enough to fill the sudden emptiness in her. She was sure of it.

His telephone rang once... twice... three times.

By now, Joelle was having second thoughts about what she was doing. Maybe it would only make things worse.

Suddenly someone lifted the receiver, and Joelle stopped breathing.

"Hello," a woman said, her distinct Cajun accent being very similar to what Joelle remembered of Gabriel's. Only hers was more pronounced, and she sounded much older than Gabriel. Old enough, in fact, for Joelle to wonder if it was his mother. It was the only thing that kept her stomach from bottoming out at the sound of a female voice answering his telephone. After all, she was only assuming that he'd been telling her the truth in Acapulco when he'd said he was single and unattached.

Suddenly Joelle realized that there was always the possibility that the information that Gabriel Lafleur had told her about himself in Mexico was, in fact, a lie. *Maybe he was married. Maybe he even had kids.* The thought nearly paralyzed her and her mouth went dry.

"Who is this?" the woman asked, indignantly. "Is this some kind of a prank call? 'Cause if it is..."

Joelle swallowed. "No—this is not a prank call," she finally said after finding her voice. "I'm sorry if I gave you that impression."

"Then, who's this?"

"I—I'm Joelle Ames."

"Are you selling somethin'? 'Cause if you are, I ain't buyin'."

"Uh—no. I'm not with a telemarketing service."

"Hmm... Is that so? Then, who do you want to speak to?"

"W-well, actually..." Joelle said, stammering her words. The woman was certainly intimidating her. "I think I may have dialed the wrong number."

"What number did you want?" the woman asked, briskly.

"Uh..." Shaken Joelle glanced down at the telephone number Gabriel had given her. With trembling fingers, she lifted the piece of paper and read off the ten-digit number, area code included.

"Well, you got the right number," the older woman said. "So, if it ain't me you want, then I guess it's Gabe."

Gabe? Short for Gabriel. Well, at least he'd given her his correct name and telephone number. Her stomach settled down—somewhat. Hopefully every-thing else he'd said about himself was true, too. Oth-erwise, she was going to hate herself even more for what she'd done with him.

Joelle cleared her throat. "As a matter of fact, I did call to speak to Gabriel," Joelle replied.

"Well, he ain't come in from the fields just yet. I'm Big Sadie, his housekeeper. I'll tell him you called."

Joelle already knew she'd made a mistake in phon-ing him and decided that this was her last chance to pull out.

"That's quite all right. In fact, I'd prefer if you didn't even tell him anything. Please, just forget that I called. I'm sorry to have disturbed you. Goodbye."

"Now wait a minute, *cher*. I think I know who you are."

"I doubt that," Joelle replied.

"Well, let me see, now... I bet you, you're that woman he met on vacation."

Joelle's grip on the receiver tightened. "He told you about me?" she asked, in truth, awed down to her toes that Gabriel would even do such a thing.

His housekeeper smirked. "Well, that ain't exactly how it was. See, I saw them pictures he took of you, and he said that you were his tour partner—or some-thin' like that. Anyways, I ain't never seen Gabe take so many pictures of anyone."

Joelle frowned to herself. Funny, but she didn't re-call Gabriel taking any snapshots of her in Acapulco. Oh—well, yeah, maybe one or two that she'd no-ticed. Mostly she'd seen him taking pictures of the scenery. Sometimes that scenery may have been lo-cated behind her. Therefore, if by chance she ended up in any of those snapshots, then it was purely by accident.

"Oh—look—don't hang up," the housekeeper said. "I think I hear Gabe comin' in now." A fraction of a moment later and much too soon for Joelle to have stopped her, Joelle heard when the older woman laid the receiver down and said, "It's for you, Gabe."

Joelle's insides froze.

"Who is it?" he asked.

"That woman?"

"What woman?" Joelle heard Gabriel ask.

"The one in the pictures."

"Pictures?"

"The ones from your vacation."

"Oh—those pictures." There was a long pause and then finally Gabriel said, "I'll take it in my study."

Joelle's heart began to pound once again.

She certainly had plenty of time to hang up and even thought of doing so. But then she realized it would only make her look like an even bigger fool, so she took a couple of deep breaths and waited anxiously for him to answer. Finally she heard him say, "Hello."

Air rushed from her lungs. "Gabriel?"

There was a momentary pause. "Yes."

"This is Joelle. Joelle Ames..." Actually there was always the chance that he wouldn't remember her. Or, at least, her name. The sudden thought that he might not caused something in her to shrivel up like plastic wrapping in a hot oven.

"Hello, Joelle," he said, his tone of voice even and unemotional. "I was beginning to wonder if I was ever going to hear from you, again."

She tried swallowing down the lump in her throat.

"Look, maybe my calling you like this wasn't such a good idea, after all," Joelle replied. "I probably should've let my attorney do this."

"But you called instead," he said.

"Well—yes—but—"

"But, what?"

"Nothing," Joelle replied, suddenly realizing that she was getting paranoid for nothing. Sure, if she were to tell him about the baby, he would probably freak out. But she wasn't going to do that. She'd just called to talk to him . . . to hear his voice one more time. She didn't plan to ever call him, again.

"Look," he drawled, "I've been meaning to phone you. In fact, I was wondering if your attorney had turned up anything about—well, you know—about that night."

Joelle took a deep, steadying breath. "Well, actually, that's why I called." *Liar.* "I wanted to let you know that he hasn't been able to find anything, no documentation that we got married. No nothing. Lately he's been saying that we might not ever know what really happened that night."

"I see," Gabriel replied, hesitantly. "In that case, what do you suggest we do?"

"I don't know," she said. "What do you think?"

"Well, it's been well over a month now. If there is still no documentation to be found, I don't see the point in either of us pursuing the matter. It looks to me like we obviously backed out of what we had planned when we left the cantina."

Yeah, they'd just ended up in bed together, instead. And she had the proof of what they'd done growing inside of her.

"I think you're probably right. I sure hope so," Joelle said, coolly. But, in spite of her indifferent answer, her stomach sank to the floor.

"I hope so, too," he replied. "Look, I think it's time we just consider the whole incident dropped."

"Sounds good to me," Joelle said, forcing herself to sound as elated as he. "Besides, if a problem should result, I'll have my attorney take care of it right away."

For a long moment, Gabriel was silent. Finally, he cleared his throat. "Listen, now that I've had a moment to think about it, just to put both of our minds at ease, maybe we should sign some kind of an agreement, naming each other blameless for that night."

Joelle stiffened. It wasn't that she wanted anything from him, because she didn't. It was the fact that he was suddenly so suspicious of her. As if he thought that she had some underlying motive in all of this. In truth, she could've been thinking the very same thing of him, but she wasn't. "Look, Lafleur, let's get one thing straight. I'm not one to cause you any problems, okay?"

"In that case, you shouldn't mind my asking you to sign an agreement."

"Not at all," she replied, irritably.

"Good. Give me the name of your attorney and I'll have my lawyer contact yours."

"Fine," Joelle said in a tight voice. She spouted out the name of her attorney and his telephone number. Next she looked up his address just to make sure her memory was correct and then gave it to Gabriel. After a short pause, she said, "Is there anything else I can do for you before I hang up?"

"Ames," he said, "there's no point in getting upset over this."

"I'm not."

"It's just a formality."

"Fine. Have your attorney draw up the document, mail it to me and I'll sign it."

"It's nothing personal."

"Of course, not."

"Look, you probably have as much to lose in this as I do."

"Probably more," Joelle stated.

"Then, why do I get this feeling—"

Joelle cleared her throat. "There's no reason why you and I have to speak again. From this point on, I'll have my attorney handle my affairs in this matter."

"But—"

"I hope you will extend the same courtesy to me that I plan to give you."

"Of course," he said, abruptly.

"Good," Joelle replied.

And then a moment later *click!* she hung up the receiver.

Turning away from the telephone, she released a deep sigh.

She never, ever wanted to see or hear from that man again. He was infuriating. He didn't deserve to know about the baby she was carrying, therefore, she was quite happy that she hadn't experienced a moment of weakness and told him.

Besides, if she had, undoubtedly he would've thought that she'd gotten pregnant on purpose.

Her phone rang almost immediately. Startled, and still too shaken from her conversation with Gabriel, she let her answering machine pick up.

"Joelle? This is Gabriel. I know you're there.... Listen, I want to talk to you."

Her heart began to pound in her chest.
Like hell, if she would talk to him again.
She'd heard all she needed to hear from him.
She wasn't calling him back for anything. Not ever.

Chapter Three

Gabriel Lafleur had no earthly idea why he'd come all the way to California to see Joelle Ames. It had been two months now since their infamous night together in Acapulco. One month since that night he'd gotten that unexpected telephone call from her. He'd tried several times after that to reach her, but she'd never returned any of his messages. Her avoidance of him had only fueled his growing suspicions, so in the end, he'd gotten his own attorney to check out that night in Mexico, only to have the man say he couldn't find anything. Gabriel knew it should've been enough for him to put some kind of closure to the whole affair, but it wasn't.

In fact, regardless of his constant efforts to the contrary, he still thought about her all the time.

It was driving him crazy the way her memory seemed to have gotten a hold on him. Crazier still because if there was one woman in this whole world that he knew was all wrong for him, it was Joelle Ames.

After hailing a cab and giving the driver her address, it wasn't any time at all before he was getting out at the curb near her high-rise apartment complex. He rode the elevator up to her floor, found her apartment number and knocked on her door.

Within moments, she opened it, wearing a pale pink bathrobe and matching slippers. She looked just the way he remembered her, and his eyes gobbled up the sight of her.

"Hello, Ames," he said. He couldn't help but notice that his heart had begun to pound wildly. Too wildly, in fact, for a mere social call.

"Lafleur," she replied, surprise evident in her voice. She licked nervously at the corners of her mouth and as a result his stomach bottomed out. "W-what are you doing here?"

"May I come in?"

She hesitated momentarily and then stepped to one side. "Come in," she finally said.

"Did I catch you at a bad time?"

Her eyes darted momentarily to a small stack of clothes she had folded on the sofa. Slipping past him, she headed in that direction. "Uh—no, that's all right," she said. She picked up the clothes rather hastily and started for a doorway that Gabriel presumed led to a rear bedroom. "I'll just put these away," she added with a nervous-looking smile on her face.

It was easy to see that she wasn't all that happy to see him. He probably should've called first before showing up at her door. Truthfully he had been raised to have better manners than that.

What was he doing here, anyway?

Gabe watched as Joelle slipped through the doorway and saw when she dropped a piece of clothing from the stack she was carrying. He immediately went to pick it up and then called out to get her attention. She turned around and came back. "What is it?" she asked, pulling her eyebrows into a frown.

"You dropped this," Gabe said, and for the first time he actually looked down at what he held in his hand and saw it was a drawstring nightgown. The kind that newborn babies sometimes wear. He frowned. "I didn't know you had a kid."

"I don't," Joelle said, quickly taking the nightgown from him. "It belongs to a friend of mine. I—uh—I do her laundry sometimes to help her out."

"Oh," he replied.

"I'll be right back," she told him.

He nodded.

While she was gone, Gabe gazed around Joelle's den, admiring her taste in decorating. Everything looked brand spanking new—and expensive. She had class, lots of it. But then he had known that the first time he'd laid eyes on her in the hotel lobby in Acapulco. That day she'd had on a light blue business suit and black leather pumps, and her light brown hair had been twisted in a knot behind her head. Even then, he had known she wasn't his type. In fact, he'd been totally surprised the following day when he'd found out that she was a tourist like himself. He'd figured she was in Acapulco on business. And when the tour guide had paired them off as partners later that afternoon, he'd been even more surprised when they'd hit it off from the start. Still, it wasn't hard to recognize that they were total opposites in both personality and lifestyle, and gazing at all the pretty, undisturbed items in her fancy high-fashioned apartment only proved it. It was the complete opposite from the ageless beauty of his old plantation house.

It took Joelle longer than he expected for her to return, and it gave him a moment to think of how odd it was for him to be standing here, waiting for her. He'd never thought he'd stand around waiting for a woman ever again in his life. His ex-wife, he'd thought, had seen to that. But, in spite of himself, for the past two months now, he found that Joelle Ames was all he thought about. In more ways than he cared to admit, she'd become almost like a dream to him.

Only now she was within his grasp, and he could hardly believe it.

Not that he planned on touching her while he was here.

Not that he actually wanted to.

Well, actually, he did want to. But he knew better. Touching her, even once, even lightly on the arm, would've been his undoing.

Ah, to hell with all this craziness inside of him, Gabe told himself a moment later. After all, he'd only come here to find a way to put some closure to the time they'd spent together. To begin with, the very last thing he wanted as a permanent fixture in his life was a woman. He'd learned the hard way that they were nothing but trouble and heartache. And, frankly, he didn't need either.

Joelle finally reentered the room. "I'm sorry to have kept you waiting," she said. "If only you had called first, I would've—"

"I know," he said, bowing his head for just a moment. "I should've called first. But to be honest with you, I didn't want to."

"Oh," she said. "Well, after I didn't return any of your phone messages, I guess I had that coming."

He smiled. "Why didn't you return any of my calls?"

He watched as she inhaled deeply and then released it. "I don't know," she said at the end of her breath. "I guess I couldn't see the point."

"I see," he replied.

She licked her lips self-consciously.

Gabe watched as she did so and then swallowed. Those lips of hers were driving him crazy. Good grief, what was she trying to do to him, anyway? Gut him wide open with the tip of her tongue?

"Look, Ames..."

"Lafleur, we both said we needed to get on with our lives..."

"Exactly," he replied.

"Well, I have," she said.

"I have, too," he replied. "Well, sort of..."

Damn, Gabriel thought, but he didn't know what to say. He couldn't even give her a reason for coming all this way to see her.

Had he really come all this way just to see her?

Now that was ridiculous.

Only an idiot would do such a thing.

He was, in fact, an idiot.

A complete idiot.

What in the hell did he want from this woman, anyway?

Well...actually, that was the strange part. He wanted nothing, absolutely nothing from her but for her to leave him alone.

Right?

He was an idiot.

Big time.

"I was wondering if you'd like to have dinner with me tonight," he said.

She frowned skeptically as though she didn't believe for one minute that that was his reason for looking her up. "Why are you here, Lafleur? Have you decided that we need to sign that document, after all?"

"Document?" Gabe asked, but then he remembered what she was talking about. "Oh—that. No, that's not why I'm here. After we spoke that time on the phone I had my attorney check matters out in Mexico and he came up with the same conclusion as your attorney did."

"He found nothing, right?"

"Right," he replied.

"Then I don't understand why you're here."

Rubbing the back of his neck to relieve some of the tension, Gabe sighed. "To be perfectly honest with you, I don't have any idea why I'm here. If, anything, call it gut instinct. It's as though something inside of me—like a hunch—keeps me at odds about what happened that night."

"Well," Joelle said, her eyes widening. Suddenly she bit down on her bottom lip and seemed almost...frightened. "I can't imagine what that could be."

"No," he said, watching her closely, "neither can I."

She turned and walked stiffly toward the door, giving him a clear indication that she wanted him to leave.

Well, he wasn't ready to go yet. Something told him that if he just stuck this out a little longer, he'd have the answers he came for. He walked right up to her. "Look, Ames, I wish I could just walk away from this, but I can't. I've got this weird feeling inside and it just doesn't go away."

She stepped back from him and it was obvious that she was really trying to avoid him now. Like she *did* have something she was trying to hide. And, damned that feeling inside him just grew even stronger.

Joelle glanced up and their eyes met.

And suddenly it was as though the air in the room decompressed.

Gabe's eyes narrowed. "What are you hiding, Ames?"

"I'm not hiding anything," she said, breathlessly.

"Then why do I get this feeling that you are?"

"I have no idea."

Suddenly a whistle went off in another room.

Joelle jumped in surprise and then glanced back in the direction of the sound. "I—uh—forgot. I was boiling myself some water for a cup of tea. Uh—w-would you like some? It's decaf."

"No," Gabriel said, gruffly, frowning at her. It was just that he was so disappointed that he'd let the earlier moment slip by. For a second there, he'd seemed so close to getting some answers. "I don't drink tea. But you go ahead."

Joelle looked flustered. It was as though she didn't know if she really wanted to do that now, or what. But the whistle kept on blowing off steam and, so finally, she dashed off for the kitchen.

Gabriel followed right behind her.

She was obviously shaken, but just why he couldn't figure out. But he knew he was close to finding the answer. He could feel it.

She glanced back over her shoulder.

He smiled.

She didn't.

Yeah, he was on to something, all right. Like a bloodhound. It was time to move in for the kill.

Joelle's galley kitchen was long and narrow and had a large picture window at one end. An English ivy in a copper teakettle sat on the wood-stained windowsill. Gabe walked up to it and gazed out at the city below. Finally, with his hands in his front jean pockets, he turned with a solemn look on his face and it was then that he saw the bottle of vitamins that was placed on a shelf just above her head. For some reason, the boldly written labeling caught his eye.

After a moment, he dropped his gaze and watched as Joelle poured herself a cup of tea. Her telephone rang and she immediately excused herself to answer it in another room. Apparently she preferred not answering it in the kitchen where he was, because there was a telephone sitting on the countertop right next to where she'd been standing. Obviously her private life was her own and she planned on keeping it that way from him.

With nothing to do until she returned, Gabe walked forward and for some reason found himself inquisitive once again about the bottle of vitamins that was placed on the shelf above the sink. Narrowing his angle of vision, he began scrutinizing the labeling.

From the next room, he could hear Joelle speaking into the telephone and it sounded as if she was taking down instructions. In fact, he was almost certain she was jotting down the words as she said them out loud. "A week from tomorrow at two-thirty. My scheduled monthly appointment. Yes, I remembered. Thank you." Then she hung up.

Gabe deepened his frown as he lifted the bottle of vitamins from the shelf and began reading. The word prenatal stuck out above all the other labeling in big, bold red letters. Suddenly a huge void emptied out the pit of his stomach. Then his whole insides froze. The vitamins were prescribed to Joelle by a doctor.

Prenatal had only one meaning to him. She was pregnant.

Behind the bottle of vitamins were several brochures, the kind found in most doctor offices. They were all on pregnancy. One was on good nutrition, the other just gave general information about a fetus in the early stages of development. After quickly scanning them, he replaced the brochures on the shelf. The bottle of prenatal vitamins, however, he still held in his hands. By now his heart was pounding out of control.

It couldn't be.

Surely she would've told him in Mexico if she were going to have a baby. Maybe these weren't actually hers. Maybe she had a roommate.

Not if they've been prescribed in her name, stupid. Get a grip. They're hers.

Damn, why was it so difficult for him to want to believe that? Just because he'd spent a few days—and one passion-filled night—with this woman didn't mean he knew everything there was to know about her. In fact, he knew very little and was beginning to realize that by the minute.

He'd made love to her in Mexico while she'd been pregnant by another man.

He didn't know why, but, frankly, he was floored.

And, for some unknown reason, downright bothered with that idea.

She should've told him.

Gabe's frown deepened. Just where in the hell was the father of this kid, anyway? Not that it was really any of his business, he knew. And yet, for some reason, he damned sure felt it was. It was eating at his gut like crazy to know that she'd been on the rebound from another man when he'd first met her.

And she was going to have this man's baby.

In that moment Joelle walked back into the room and froze when she saw what he held in his hand. "Just what do you think you're doing, Lafleur," she managed between clenched teeth. "Give me that," she demanded a moment later, rushing forward and yanking the bottle from his hand. Her expression was as brittle as ice. "You've invaded my privacy long enough and now I think it's time you leave."

It was her attitude that piqued Gabe's curiosity more than anything and got that feeling of his all fired up, again. What was the big deal if he knew she was pregnant?

By now, a million thoughts were flying through his head. He wanted some answers, by golly. He'd come too far to just turn around and leave now.

"Who's the father?" he asked.

She ignored him and replaced the bottle of vitamins on the shelf. Her hand was trembling.

He leaned forward and whispered near her ear. "I asked, who is the father?"

"That's none of your business, Lafleur," she snapped back from over her shoulder. "Now please leave."

Gabe's heart was pounding. His first wife hadn't wanted children, but he had wanted an heir. He still did, only obtaining one the good old-fashioned way, by getting remarried, simply wasn't the answer for him, anymore. In fact, he'd had many a sleepless night over this dilemma with no feasible resolution in sight. And now to discover that the woman he'd made such mad, passionate love with while on vacation was pregnant was hitting too close to home. He knew what the odds were of it being his kid. Remote, at best. He just needed her to verify that by saying who the father was.

"Just tell me the father's name," Gabe said, placing his hands on his hips. He wasn't going to let her get away from him until she did.

Visibly shaken, Joelle shook her head. "There's no point in me telling you that," she said. "He and I have already gone our separate ways. And, besides, it's none of your business."

"I see," Gabe replied, still unrelenting in his pursuit for inner peace. He decided to ignore her last comment. "Does he know about the baby?"

Joelle sighed heavily. "Look, he didn't in the beginning, but he does now."

"And . . . ?" Gabriel asked.

"And, what?"

"And is he going to take full responsibility?"

Joelle's features went blank. "He doesn't care about me or the baby—which is for the best."

Gabriel gaped at her. "How could you sleep with a guy like that?"

"I guess I'm just plain stupid," she said, tightly.

"Did you love him?"

"No," she said, and it was the first time she actually looked him in the face since this whole conversation had started. It was as though she was trying hard to make a point with him.

"Who broke up with who?"

"What is this, Lafleur, the third degree?" she asked. Then, drawing in a deep breath, she seemed to resign herself to the fact that she was going to have to answer his questions if she wanted to get rid of him. "Look, it was mutual, okay?"

"That's pretty tough," he said.

She removed the tea bag from her cup. He noticed that her hands were still trembling. She must have really cared about this guy, he thought.

"It would've never worked out between us," Joelle replied. "I knew that from the very beginning, and so did he."

"So, you've decided to raise your baby alone?"

"That's right."

"Without a father?"

"That's right. Look, I grew up without a mother and I survived."

"But did you like it?" he asked.

She hesitated for the longest time. "No—not particularly. But..."

"But, what?" Gabe asked, wanting to pursue his line of questioning until she gave him some answers. Some *real* answers.

It looked as if she was still as determined in life not to have a husband as he was not to have a wife. Well, he could understand that. Of course, their reasons for that were as different as night and day. He'd been hurt by his ex-wife's betrayal. She simply wanted to be a full-time career woman—and, obviously, still did—and he couldn't help but wonder how this unexpected pregnancy was going to fit into her plans. Certainly it must have knocked a big kink into them.

Joelle folded her arms across her chest. "Look, Lafleur, you're really trying my patience."

Yeah, Gabe thought, he probably was. It just seemed such a shame that she was going to have a baby for a man whom she said couldn't care less. Gabe couldn't imagine how any man could've just turned his back and walked away from that kind of responsibility. No wonder today's world was in such a mess. Everyone wanted to have the fun, but no one wanted to pay the consequences.

Well, he wasn't raised that way. If Joelle had been carrying his baby, he knew exactly what he would've done. He would've tackled that responsibility head-on, regardless of the price. And there would've been a price, of course. Nothing in life came without one. But, frankly, where he came from, when it came to matters of this nature, a man had no choice but to do what was right.

Joelle released a deep breath and then stepped toward the doorway leading back to the front of her apartment. "Look, I have an appointment in less than an hour and I'm not even dressed yet. I'm sorry, but you're going to have to leave now."

Gabe smirked knowingly. Somehow he doubted if she really did have an appointment, but at the same time, he knew he'd already overstayed, if not overstated, his visit. It was time to go—for now, at least.

"About dinner tonight," he said.

"I have plans," she replied, tightly.

Gabriel doubted that, too. But if need be, he could be a patient man, for a while.

"Lunch tomorrow?"

"I can't."

"I see. Well, in that case, I may be in town longer than I expected. Look, I'll call you later. Maybe you'll have found some free time by then."

They had reached her front door. "I doubt it," she replied.

Gabe grinned. He wanted her to know he saw right through her.

"Look, what do you want from me?" Joelle asked.

"Actually," he said, "I don't want anything from you, exactly. I just want to get rid of this nagging feeling inside that something isn't quite right. I thought coming out here and talking to you face-to-face would do it for me, but it hasn't."

She licked those full lips of hers, again.

His stomach did a wild somersault. The woman could certainly charge up his libido.

"I wish I could help you," she said with a shrug. "But I can't."

Gabriel shook his head. Maybe she was right, he told himself. Maybe he had been wrong in coming to her for answers. After all, whatever was bugging him was his problem, not hers.

He inhaled deeply. "I'm sorry. I shouldn't have barged in on your life this way. I've been a real jerk."

"Don't worry about it," she replied.

He nodded, then offered her his hand. "Well, then I guess this is goodbye—for good, this time."

After pausing momentarily, she took it. "Yes, I guess it is."

A few seconds later he stepped into the hallway and she closed the door behind him. Turning for one more glance of her apartment, he released a deep breath. Then he headed for the elevator.

He was a lucky man, he told himself. If Joelle Ames wasn't such an independent woman, she certainly could've created some serious problems for him. She could've easily deceived him by saying that he was the baby's father and, under the circumstances, he would've probably believed her.

Indeed, he was a lucky man. He was off the hook.

So why, then, didn't he feel that way? Why was that nagging feeling persisting?

But more importantly, why, he wondered, hadn't he bothered to notice the date on that prescription of prenatal vitamins? It sure could've set his mind at ease.

Dammit, he had to find something that would.

And he wasn't leaving San Diego until he did.

Shaken to the core, Joelle caught her breath as she leaned momentarily against her closed door. It was the first time since allowing Gabriel to walk into her apartment that she'd been able to breathe with ease. Thank heaven, he was gone.

That was a close call, she thought to herself. Too close, in fact. She'd had to think quickly to cover her tracks when he'd discovered her bottle of vitamins. And what about the infant gown she'd been unable to resist buying? Of all the items to have dropped on the floor, practically at his feet!

Oh, God, but she hoped that he believed her story. He probably had . . .

Yes, of course he had, she told herself a moment later. He'd come here looking for answers to a nagging doubt he'd had and she'd given him the out he was looking for. Undoubtedly, once that sunk in, he was going to gladly accept it and go back home.

She didn't need him, anyway. She didn't need anyone. She was quite capable of having this baby and a full-time career all at the same time. She saw other women doing it, and they made it look like a breeze. Therefore, if they could, she could.

She was sure of it.

Well . . . she wasn't that sure of it. There would be some problems, of course. For example, eventually she would have to move into a bigger place. Something with a backyard for the baby to play in. And she would have to find a reliable, live-in sitter and, considering how particular she was, that probably was going to be a problem. Truthfully it was still incredible to her that she was going to have a baby.

Gabriel's baby.

But it didn't matter that he was the father. This was her baby and she didn't feel in the least bit guilty for not telling him. After all, she had her rights, too, and like him, she didn't want any problems.

Why, then, if that was the case, her inner voice replied, did she feel so lonely, so unsure of her future now that he had come and gone once more from her life? Why did a part of her want to call him back?

Because that part of her was the weak, vulnerable woman she kept hidden from the world. Sometimes, even from herself. Her father had always ridiculed a helpless woman as being worthless to society. And when she allowed that part of herself to show, she couldn't help it. She felt worthless.

Still and all, she hoped she was doing the right thing by not telling Gabriel about the baby. It wasn't that she wanted to be deceitful, or cruel. Her pregnancy had turned her whole life upside-down and everything was just so confusing for her right now. What had once been her top priorities in life were now lying painfully on the floor. She was doing the best she could.

Besides, what would Gabriel have done, if he had known about the baby? Offer her money?

She didn't need his money.

Love?

No way. He'd made it quite plain to her how he felt about that when they were together in Mexico. He didn't want a wife, he'd said. And, of course, she'd said she didn't want a husband. And she still didn't. She wanted a career. It was important to her. She would somehow—hopefully—work the baby into her busy schedule. But, a demanding husband? Uh-uh. No way.

And it didn't matter that Gabriel Lafleur was the first and only man to ever touch her soul—even momentarily. The thing she had to remember was, indeed, it had been for only a moment.

Besides, women didn't get respect for being in love with a man. They got it for working their way to the top position of a major corporation.

And that was her goal in life. And she wasn't going to let anyone or anything stop her. She'd already made her decision. On Monday morning, she was going to accept the position offered to her by one of Southern California's leading advertising firms.

Her baby's future was secured, right here in San Diego.

Chapter Four

Gabriel boarded the elevator on Joelle's floor and started down.

Dammit, but he couldn't seem to let go of this crazy feeling that something just didn't add up.

She wasn't having his kid, he said to himself a moment later in the hopes that might put things into its proper perspective.

But it didn't.

Dammit, it wasn't his kid, he repeated to himself.

It still didn't help.

Nothing did.

His gut was boiling with uncertainty.

Her story made sense and, yet, it didn't.

He wanted to believe her and, yet, he couldn't quite bring himself to do that.

First off, he felt certain he would've somehow known if she had been pregnant in Mexico. If nothing else, she had been so open with him, Joelle would've told him herself.

Gabriel drew in a deep breath and then released it. Ah, the hell with it, he thought. She wanted him out of her life, therefore, he was getting the hell out of her life. Right?

Right.

He frowned. So, go ahead, Lafleur, and get the heck out of her life like she wants you to.

The elevator stopped on the bottom floor and the doors opened. But by now his feet were like lead weights and he couldn't have stepped from the elevator in that moment if his life had depended on it.

His mouth was parched dry.

His hands trembled.

No way could he leave like this. It went against every grain in his body. Something just didn't add up and he had to know what.

He punched the elevator button back up to her floor.

This time he was going to get the truth from her, once and for all.

And this time he wasn't going to leave without it.

Joelle heard the outrageous pounding on her door and for a moment was alarmed. But then she heard Gabriel's voice. Without a second thought, she pulled open the door. "What's wrong, for heaven's sake?"

Gabriel came barreling into her apartment as if he had every right to. "H-has something happened?" she stammered.

"I want to see that bottle of prenatal vitamins," he said, heading for her kitchen.

With pulses racing, Joelle stepped ahead of him, blocking his path. "You don't have the right to barge in here like this," she stated.

He looked her straight in the eyes. "I damned sure do. We slept together in Mexico, remember? Therefore, I have every right."

"That's absurd," she argued, and when he tried to go around her, she held out her arms and blocked the doorway leading to the kitchen. "Get out of here, Lafleur."

Halting, he placed his hands on his hips and glared at her. "I'm not leaving, Ames. So you just as soon give me some answers I can believe. Because frankly, until now, you haven't.

"In fact," he said a moment later, "let's forget about all the formalities this time around. Are you carrying my baby?"

Joelle's hand flew to her chest. Her knees became like pudding and for a moment she thought she might just slip to the floor. "Oh, my God," she said, "who told you that?"

He stepped forward. "Then it is my baby?"

Fortunately for Joelle, she was able to regain a fragment of her composure. But only a fragment. "No—no, that's not what I meant."

His eyes narrowed. "Then what exactly do you mean?"

"This baby is mine," she exclaimed.

"That's not an answer to my question and you know it. Who's the father, Ames?"

"That's none of your business."

"It damned sure is, considering the fact that this kid could be mine. How many weeks are you?"

His words were angry but, in spite of that, Joelle didn't feel she was in any physical danger from him. "Like I said," she remarked, haughtily, "that's none of your business."

"You weren't pregnant in Mexico, were you?"

Refusing to answer, Joelle glared at him.

"Look, I have every right to know if this baby is mine."

"You don't have any right to my private affairs," she said defiantly.

"If you wanted privacy, then you should've kept your head in Mexico."

Her mouth dropped open. "How dare you."

"How dare you think you have the right to keep something like this from me. Am I the father of your baby?" he asked insistently.

Joelle's composure was in shambles at her feet and she was left trembling with indecision. She couldn't take much more pressure and knew if he continued to apply it with such strength, it would be only a matter of time before she gave in. And that's the last thing she wanted to do.

"Look," Gabriel said, drawing in a deep breath. "I deserve the truth and you know it."

Tears stung for the first time in Joelle's eyes. "Why can't you just leave well enough alone?"

"Because that's not the way I am," he replied, his voice slipping somewhat. "All you have to do to get rid of me is to tell me that I'm wrong. So, go ahead, Ames. Just tell me flat out that I'm wrong. That this is not my baby you're having."

Joelle's mouth trembled. "And what if it is?" she said in a whisper.

Air gushed out from Gabriel's lungs. "Oh, God, then it is my baby, isn't it?"

Joelle felt cornered. Her heart was aching and she felt so vulnerable, so defenseless in that moment that she couldn't even bring herself to continue lying to him. "Yes," she finally whispered, her voice hoarse with emotion.

She saw when Gabriel shivered from the shock of actually hearing her admit the truth. Unable to handle the stark, bare moment, Joelle closed her eyes and tried to regain control of herself.

Eventually, when she felt strong enough to open them, she looked at him. He was still gaping at her. Well, he'd wanted the truth. So, now he had it. "Okay, Lafleur, so now you know the truth. I'd like for you to leave."

"What?"

"You heard me. Just go—please."

He gaped at her. "You can't be serious."

"Well, I am."

He grabbed her by the upper arms. "Then, you're crazy if you think I'm just going to turn around and walk away without one single thought to the fact that you're having my baby."

"Why not? Some men do."

"Well, not me," he said, suddenly letting go of her. As if he didn't want to have to touch her a moment longer.

"There's no need for you to be so gallant, Lafleur. We're in the last decade of the twentieth century, for heaven's sake. As of this moment, consider yourself off the hook. I'm assuming full responsibility for this pregnancy."

His dark, intense gaze leveled on her face and then slowly began dropping down her body until they reached her abdomen. "You can forget that idea. I'm as responsible for what's happened as you are. Not only that, but I want this baby."

Joelle felt as if someone had just punched her in the stomach. She had known if he found out, he'd cause her problems. Men always seemed to cause her problems. "What do you mean?"

"This baby is my heir."

"It's mine, too."

Joelle couldn't believe what he was saying. When she'd met him in Acapulco, he'd been so different, so fun-loving. "B-but in Mexico, you said..."

"I said a lot of things in Mexico. And so did you. And if I remember correctly, having kids of your own wasn't in your future plans."

"Nor yours, for that matter. You said you never wanted to marry, again."

"And I never planned to," he remarked, running frustrated fingers through his hair. "But then I never planned on you getting pregnant, either."

Joelle tilted her chin slightly higher. "Well, neither did I."

"Okay," Gabriel said, releasing a deep breath. "Let's stop right here and face facts. It seems that neither of us was expecting this. But it's happened, so now we have to take full responsibility for it."

"That," Joelle replied, defiantly, "is exactly what I'm doing. And I don't need help from anyone. Not even you."

Joelle could tell he was frustrated with her by the way he kept running his fingers through his hair.

"Look," he said, "could we possibly sit down and discuss this calmly like two sensible adults?"

Joelle knew without a doubt that she should've insisted that he leave and that she would regret it soon if she didn't. Still, as ridiculous as it was, for some reason having him know about the baby seemed to have released some of the stress—not to mention, a large quantity of the guilt—she'd been carrying around on her shoulders for the past month. It was almost comforting to have him know her secret. Other than herself and her doctor, he was the only other person who did. And she supposed there was a kind of righteousness in that fact. She had felt guilty for not telling him about the baby. But, at the same time, she had been trying to avoid just the kind of complication they were presently having.

"Please," he said, again, "can't we sit down?"

Without actually replying, Joelle sat down on the edge of a chair. Gabriel quickly followed her lead and sat on the sofa opposite her.

"Look," he said, starting off the conversation, "I can't just ignore the fact that you're going to have my baby. I know this isn't something we planned, but I can't see that you and I have any other alternative now but to do what's right. We can't just assume any more about what we did that night in Mexico. We'll have to get married again, here in the States."

Joelle's stomach knotted. "That's ridiculous. You and I don't have to get married at all, just because I'm pregnant. Besides, you said that you didn't want a wife, remember?"

"And you don't want a husband. But that's beside the point now. You're pregnant, and that's that."

"To you, maybe, but not to me."

"Look, I want my baby to have my name—legally. It's important to me."

"Oh—well—and an hour ago you didn't even know this baby existed. And now all of a sudden it's all that important to you that he carry your name?"

"Exactly," he replied.

Joelle frowned. "Why weren't you that concerned about the possible consequences that night in Mexico?"

"The same as you, I guess. I was drunk and just plain stupid. We made a mistake."

"That's no excuse," Joelle replied.

"You're right. It isn't. We have no excuse for what we did. But, is the baby we made that night going to have to pay for that?"

Joelle's frown deepened. "I can't believe this baby means that much to you," she exclaimed in self-defense.

Gabriel's features went blank. "Well, you'd better start believing it. In fact, I'm ready to do whatever I have to in order to claim this baby as mine. And if that means having a wife in the process, then so be it."

The nerve of the guy, Joelle thought. "Well, I don't want a husband," she said.

"Well, I don't really want a wife. But that's just too bad. Unlike you, I care enough about this baby to be willing to make the necessary sacrifice for his well-being."

Blood rushed to Joelle's face. He was implying that she was being selfish.

A moment later, she jumped to her feet. "I don't have to take this from you," she cried out. But, in spite of her argument to the contrary, a profound feeling of guilt slowly oozed through her.

Oh, great, Joelle thought, now he was trying to manipulate her—and succeeding.

"I know my showing up here like this has been a shock for you," he said with a hint of compassion in his voice. "Obviously you need time to sort your feelings out. Why don't I leave you alone for now and—"

"Don't come back." Joelle cut in.

Gabriel actually smiled at her insistence before continuing. "I'll be back, Ames, you can count on that."

Joelle frowned. "What can I do to get you off my back?"

"That's simple enough. I want my baby."

Joelle gaped at him. "You can't expect me to just give you this child."

"Unfortunately I realize that would be asking too much of you."

"How thoughtful you are of my feelings," she replied, sarcastically.

"Look, the only solution I can come up with is for us to get married and for you to come live with me in Louisiana."

Joelle actually found the resources to laugh. "You can't be serious. I have a career here and I'm not just going to throw that away."

"Why should you have to? You can have a career anywhere."

"I don't want a career anywhere. I want a career right here in San Diego."

"Where are you working now?"

That question stumped Joelle right quick. If all went well, she'd have a job by the end of next week. But at this very moment, she was still—technically—

unemployed. "Uh... I'm not, exactly." She replied, licking her lips nervously.

"Then I don't understand what it is you feel you have to lose by coming with me and starting your career over in Louisiana."

Plenty, Joelle thought to herself. Once again, her heart was pounding in her throat. She just wasn't sure what it would be plenty of and, truthfully, she was afraid to find out.

"Look..." Gabriel said, rising to his feet. "I know you said that you have plans for tonight, but, considering the circumstances, cancel them and have dinner with me."

For some reason, Joelle followed the slow movement of his body and groaned inwardly. She hated the way watching him sometimes made her feel all crazy and out of control. That, too, was frightening for her.

"I don't have any plans for tonight," Joelle said, resigning herself to the fact that she could live with her conscience a whole lot better when she was being completely honest with him.

Well, maybe not completely honest. She would never tell him about the way he sometimes made her feel inside. That would only make her look... needy.

He grinned—actually, grinned at her.

Her heart went *k-plunk*.

Silly, silly her for letting that happen.

Her well-organized life was simply falling apart at the seams and she couldn't do anything to prevent it from happening.

Still and all, there was one thing she knew she could never lose sight of—no matter what—and that was the fact that it was his baby, and not her, that he was all fired up about. He wanted an heir. Not a wife.

Not her.

She was just the excess baggage that he didn't quite know what to do with.

But, then, she didn't want him, either. Right?

Right.

But maybe having dinner with him tonight wasn't such a bad idea. Between now and then, she might be able to come up with a way of convincing him once and for all that she and her baby were really okay and that his help simply wasn't needed. In other words, thanks, but no thanks.

Why did he have to turn out to be so damned chivalrous? Where was a good old-fashioned jerk when she needed one?

She was now certain of one thing. Well...maybe she'd known this all along, but just hadn't really thought about it. A simple farmer Gabriel Lafleur was not. Actually he seemed even more complex than her father, or any man she knew, for that matter. Certainly he had his own definite ideas about life. Ideas that, in truth, she had to admire.

But, still, the man was crazy if he thought she was going to go to Louisiana with him and live out her life on a farm. In fact, she shuddered at the thought. She'd never been on a farm in her life—except that one time in high school when she'd gone on a field trip to a chicken farm. Sorry, Charlie, but living in the country wasn't her style. She liked the city's fast foods—its fast pace—and its streetlights that kept the darkness—the aloneness—of night at bay. They made her career-minded life tolerable.

"Okay, I'll have dinner with you tonight," she said, point-blank.

His eyes widened slightly. "Good," he answered. "How does eight o'clock sound?"

"Perfect," she said.

His eyes suddenly dropped to her mouth, and then the air in the room was sucked up, leaving her feeling breathless. "You know," he drawled, "I was just thinking the same thing about your lips."

"My lips?" she replied in awe.

"Yeah," he said, using his finger to trace the outline of her top lip, then her bottom one. The nerve of him to turn the tables on her like this. She should've slapped his hand away, but she didn't. "Hasn't anyone ever told you that you have a perfect mouth?"

His gaze grew intense.

Joelle felt something inside her begin to tremble. "Uh . . . no, not that I can recall."

Of course, she couldn't even think straight right now, much less recall . . .

"They're sensuously shaped. I noticed that the first time we met."

"Oh."

"And so full."

"Really?" Her knees were now wobbling.

"Uh-huh. Kissable, in fact," he said, leaning forward.

Her face automatically lifted up to his.

What are you doing? a little voice inside of her said.

Joelle hadn't the foggiest idea. But she couldn't seem to stop herself.

Actually she wasn't even trying to.

And then he kissed her, softly at first, until suddenly his arms were around her and she was pressed against his hard body. Within an instant, the mood changed from heated to intense broil and she felt as if her whole self was being consumed by him.

It was just like in Mexico, she suddenly realized. One moment she was in control and, in the next, she wasn't.

Suddenly, his hands were moving over her body, touching her breasts, cupping her buttocks, pushing her even more against his hardness. His tongue was relentless in its pursuit of her inner mouth. Her tongue fought back, driven somehow to do battle with his, in spite of knowing that she couldn't win. Surrender, she knew, was inevitable. It was just a matter of when.

Then, her doorbell rang and it jarred them to their senses. Oh, God! They had almost lost it. Holding her by the upper arms, Gabriel gazed down at her as though surprised by his own behavior.

Well, he could look surprised, but he'd started it.

Dazed, Joelle stared back. Finally she blinked her eyes.

"Expecting company?" he asked, curiously.

"Uh—no," she said, shaking herself free of what had just happened between them. "It's probably my father. He's another one who doesn't call before dropping in for a visit," she added, dryly.

"I see," Gabriel replied.

The doorbell rang, again.

Joelle frowned. "Needless to have to say, he isn't a very patient man."

Gabe pulled his eyebrows together. "I gather that."

"Look," Joelle said, anxiously. "My father doesn't know about the baby yet."

Gabriel's frown deepened. "Really? Any particular reason for that."

"Only one. He wouldn't approve."

Gabriel smirked. "You're a grown woman, Ames. You have a right to live your life as you please."

"Yeah—well, tell that to my father," she replied.

"Maybe I will," Gabriel replied, evenly.

"Look, please don't say anything about the baby. When I'm ready, I want to be the one to tell him myself."

"Okay, then," he said. "I won't."

Joelle took another deep breath, turned and looked at the door. Finally she stepped forward and opened it. Immediately her father came barreling through it.

"Okay, Joelle," he said in a blistering tone of voice, "enough is enough. I've taken all I'm going to take from you. It's been two months now since you stormed away from your job. This is insubordination. It's time you forget all this nonsense of being angry with me and come back to work." Then suddenly he glanced beyond Joelle and saw Gabriel standing just behind her. "Who are you?" he demanded.

"I'm Gabriel Lafleur."

"I've never met you before, have I?" her father asked, point-blank.

"No, sir, you haven't. But, from now on, you'll be seeing a lot more of me."

Sylvan Ames's eyes widened. "Oh? And why is that, may I ask?"

"Because your daughter and I were married two months ago in Mexico and now I've come to take her back home with me."

Immediately Joelle's insides went numb and all she could do was gape at him. At his audacity in saying such a thing. He knew there wasn't any proof that the two of them had gotten married that night in Acapulco. What was he trying to do? Drive her completely over the edge?

"That's preposterous," her father exclaimed. "Joelle would never do such an irresponsible thing."

"I'm afraid you're wrong, sir. We're married, all right. Aren't we, Ames?"

"Ames?" her father said, incredibly. "You call her Ames?"

"Uh—well, yes," Gabriel said. "From habit."

Narrowing his eyes, Sylvan Ames peered at his daughter. "Is this a joke, Joelle? You're still angry with me and, therefore, you're trying to get even, right?"

"Wrong," Gabriel said before Joelle could even summon her thoughts together in order to answer for herself.

"I can explain everything," she said a moment later.

"Yeah." Gabriel cut in with an all-knowing look on his face. "Why don't you do that? Go ahead and explain everything to your father." He paused a moment, and then added, "And I mean everything, if you get my drift."

She got it all right. He was using what he knew and what her father didn't to get her to go along with him.

Joelle swallowed. "You see, we're not married—exactly. Or, at least, we're not sure if we are."

"What in the hell does that mean?" her father retorted, his face becoming flushed with anger.

"Well, you see, we got drunk together one night and—"

"You got drunk with a man you hardly knew? Just how stupid are you, Joelle?"

"We weren't exactly strangers by then," Joelle tried explaining. But she could tell she wasn't doing very well. Her father was growing more and more livid by the minute. "Anyway, when we woke up the next morning we were both wearing wedding rings, but we couldn't find a marriage certificate."

Her father was so angry, it looked as though he were having difficulty breathing. "You slept with him just like that?"

"We made a mistake, Father."

He glowered at her for the longest time until he seemed to have some kind of enlightenment. "Well, then, if there's no marriage certificate, then there's no marriage. So put the whole ugly incident behind you. Let's face it, this isn't the first time you've messed up, Joelle. If it wouldn't be for me, why even your career would be in shambles right now."

Now that hurt Joelle. Big time. Her father knew she'd earned every credit she'd ever gotten. Why couldn't he admit that to her?

Tears glistened in her eyes, but she fought them back. Her father's lack of faith in her was legendary. All her life she'd tried to please him and, heaven help her, she had never been able to.

"It's too late for that, Father. I'm going to have a baby," she heard herself saying.

"What?"

Suddenly Gabriel's arms were around her shoulders. "You heard her," he said. "She's going to have a baby. My baby."

Sylvan Ames's face turned scarlet. "Well, now, Joelle, it seems you've really messed up good this time. Even what's left of your career is going to suffer."

"It will not," she said, defensively. "I can have this baby and a career, too."

"You're so naive," he said. "You think it's that easy to raise a child. You have no idea the sacrifices I've had to make for you. You'll never be able to do this alone."

"She won't have to," Gabriel said, suddenly interrupting the exchange between Joelle and her father. "I plan to be with her every step of the way. This is my baby, too."

Sylvan Ames smirked. "Mark my word, Joelle. You've made a big mistake here, and if you don't do what's necessary to end this mess-up now, once and for all, then one day you'll be sorry you didn't take my advice."

"I'm sorry you feel that way, Mr. Ames," Gabriel said.

Getting in one final, aggravated smirk, her father finally turned and walked out.

Hurting inside, Joelle watched him go.

Because no matter what her father thought of her, she still loved him.

Chapter Five

Gabriel shut the door behind Joelle's father and frowned. "Good grief, is he always like that?"

Joelle gave him a sad nod. "Yes, I'm afraid so."

"Where's your mother?" he asked.

"She died right after I was born. She relapsed from the flu and then took pneumonia. She was too weak to fight it."

"I'm sorry."

"Yeah," she said, "I am, too."

"Both of my parents are dead, too. My mother died in a car accident, and my father died within two years. His doctor said it was from an upper respiratory infection but, personally, I think he died from loneliness. They were very close. Anyway, that was almost sixteen years ago. I was nineteen at the time."

"At least they were both there for you while you were growing up," Joelle said, perhaps now understanding just a little where Gabriel was coming from.

And he was right. Earlier she'd said she had missed not having her mother there for her. The picture she suddenly imagined of his family life was touching. In fact, she would've liked it to have been her own.

"Yes," he said with a bittersweet smile on his face, "they were." Then he gazed at her. "Look, how soon can you be packed up and ready to go back with me?"

Joelle widened her eyes. "I haven't agreed to go anywhere with you."

"Look," he said, "whether or not you like it, there's a good chance that we are already man and wife. The deed is done. We've slept together. You're pregnant. Now we have to act responsible and do what's right for the baby. Surely you agree with that."

"Well—yes—of course, when you put it that way," she said.

"Ames, I didn't agree with very much of what your father had to say, but I did agreed with one thing. It isn't easy to raise a child, especially alone. Eventually something or someone will have to suffer. I simply can't deal with the possibility that it might be my baby."

Joelle frowned. "I wouldn't let that happen."

"With so many demands on you, you might not see it."

"I plan to be a good mother."

"I'm sure you do. But the bottom line is, when at all possible, a child should have both parents present while growing up."

Joelle frowned. "Do you have any idea how outdated your ideas about parenting are?"

"Do you have any idea of how little I care if they are?" he replied, placing his hands on his hips. "I still prefer to live by my own rules, old-fashioned, or not."

Her frown deepened. Maybe it was stupid of her to think she could do this alone. In all honesty, with no experience under her belt, she knew that motherhood was going to be a difficult venture for her. Maybe Gabriel was right, after all. Maybe God had set up the creation of life in humans the way he had because he wanted there to be two doting parents—not one.

Suddenly Gabriel placed his fingers under her chin and tilted her head up so that her eyes met his. "And no matter what else you might say, Ames," he drawled, "you know it's only right for you to share this baby with me."

The air in Joelle's lungs evaporated. When he looked at her that way and said those kinds of things, her heart raced out to him and she wanted to do whatever it took, no matter the cost to her, to make him happy. It was crazy, she knew. "I don't know what to do," she said, taking a deep breath.

"Then come with me, Ames, and we'll raise our child together. If it's a career you want, my housekeeper will be more than happy to baby-sit. Our child deserves to have us both in his life."

"But you're asking me to make a lifelong commitment to a marriage neither one of us want in the first place."

He shrugged. "I guess that's just going to have to be the payback for our recklessness." But then he gave her a tentative smile. "But, to tell you the truth, now that it's happened, I'm glad I'm going to have an heir."

"Well, I'm so thrilled that everything is working out for you," she said, dryly. "I just wish I could say the same."

"Hey, I don't like the setup any more than you do, but I'll take the prize any day."

"Meaning the baby, of course," she said, making sure that her heart knew it was pounding out of control for nothing. Certainly she had no illusions that she was in any way the *prize* he was referring to.

"Exactly," he replied.

But now she knew for sure.

He came up to her and took her by the shoulders. "Look, it's up to you, Joelle. But someone is going to have to pay the piper. Is it going to be us, or our baby?"

Joelle groaned. Heaven help her, but she didn't want to have to be the one to make that decision. But from the look on Gabriel's face, he knew exactly what he was doing by allowing it to be her decision, and hers alone.

He was right, she knew. Someone was going to have to pay for their one night of reckless passion. In fact, she almost hated him in that moment for being so right.

"All right, Lafleur," she said, despairingly. "You win. When you put it that way, I don't think I could live with myself if I were to choose any other way. I'll go with you to Louisiana. I'll marry you—again, if you think that's really necessary."

"I think it is," he interjected.

"Raising a child to maturity takes a long time."

"You'll have your career to keep you busy," he replied.

Some consolation, Joelle thought. "Look, if things don't work out—"

"They will," Gabriel replied.

"How can you be so sure?"

Gabriel shrugged. "Why shouldn't they? We won't have anything to fight about like most married couples do. You'll have your life. I'll have mine."

"And what about—you know—the sleeping arrangements?"

He shrugged. "There's three bedrooms upstairs. One for me, one for you and one for the baby."

Joelle gave that a moment's thought and then shrugged. "I guess it'll work. What's the nearest city to where you are?"

"You have two choices. Either Baton Rouge, or Lafayette. Both are booming towns for employment."

"Good," Joelle said, taking a deep, steadying breath. She just wished her stomach would settle down. But for some reason, the thought of spending the next twenty years or so of her life as Gabriel's wife had her in a tailspin. She was scared. Scared of her own weakness.

She was being foolish, she told herself. If nothing else, her father's constant put-downs had made her into a tough person. She could handle Gabriel Lafleur. Once she got her full equilibrium back, he wasn't going to be any problem for her at all.

"Look," Gabriel said, gazing at her intently, "we just have to keep in mind that the baby is our sole concern."

"Don't worry," she said. "I won't forget."

"So," he said, backing away from her with a smile on his face. But, of course, he could smile. He'd won. "When can you be ready to leave?"

"Will tomorrow morning be soon enough?" she said, hypothetically. She would probably need more time, but what the heck? Everything else in her life was a mess, so why not let her departure be just as chaotic? Certainly, these days, anything less wouldn't have been normal for her.

"Hey, that would be great," he said, jumping on her suggestion like a mouse on cheese. "I'll call the airport right away and get you a ticket."

Then he took a deep breath, as though to calm himself down. "So we have a deal?" he asked, anxiously.

"Yes," she finally said, after a moment's hesitation. "We have a deal."

He grinned. "Well, I'll be damned. It's really coming true. I'm going to have my heir, after all."

No mention of a wife, mind you, Joelle reminded herself. Only his heir.

The guy really had a way of making her feel like a million dollars.

A million dollars of Monopoly money.

The following day, Joelle took one last glance back over her shoulder at San Diego before boarding the jetliner. Gabriel was close behind and carefully guided her to their seats.

She'd tried talking to her father earlier that morning, but he was still angry with her and had refused her telephone call. She'd told his faithful butler what time her flight for Louisiana was leaving the San Diego airport and she had hoped that he might've changed his mind at the last minute and come to say goodbye. But, obviously, he hadn't. In some ways, that hurt more than anything. He was her father, after all, and she wanted him to care enough about her to put his pride aside just this once. But, deep down inside, she had known it wouldn't happen. Truly, for Sylvan Ames, his pride was the very air he breathed.

Lost in those thoughts, Joelle took the window seat and was barely aware when moments later, the jetliner made a smooth lift-off. Glancing out the window at her side, she was caught completely off guard when a pang of queasiness suddenly hit her, though, in truth, this wasn't her first time being airsick. It just hadn't happened to her in a while. Obviously her pregnancy wasn't helping things.

Knowing what she needed to do, Joelle closed her eyes and breathed deeply. The seat belt sign was still on, so she couldn't just get up and make a mad dash for the lavatory at the tail end of the aircraft. She glanced at Gabriel for just a moment and saw, thank goodness, that his attention was occupied at the moment by the child seated across from him. He wasn't even aware of her current distress.

The nausea seemed to come in waves, and each wave seemed to gain more and more momentum, each time pushing farther up into her throat. As a result, her skin had grown clammy and she felt light-headed. Heaven help her, but she feared that she was going to have to use one of those bags the airline provided....

Gabriel turned suddenly, as though he intended to say something to her. Instead his eyes widened when he saw the ashen look on her face. "Hey, Ames," he said, "are you all right?"

Pulling in a slow, deep breath, she nodded, hoping her positive reply would somehow fool her queasy stomach.

It didn't however.

"You look sick," he said.

She gave him a small nod. "I am," she replied.

A moment of panic framed his face. Then he glanced up and motioned for a flight attendant.

"What is it, sir?" the flight attendant asked, rushing to his side.

"It's—uh—my wife. She's sick to her stomach."

"I see," she replied, calmly, her eyes swinging to Joelle.

The seat belt sign went off.

"I'm getting up," Joelle said, praying that once she did, she would make it to the closet-size stall at the back of the airplane.

Gabriel was on his feet in an instant and moved out of her way so she could get by.

The flight attendant took control of the situation then, ushering Joelle toward the rear and helping her get into the small compact compartment at the end of the aisle. "If you need anything," she said, "just let me know. I'm right here."

Joelle mumbled thank you and then shut the door. She was sick right away.

It wasn't all that long before someone was knocking lightly on the door and Joelle figured it was the flight attendant, checking on her. She wiped her face with a damp paper towel and then opened the door just a crack.

It was Gabriel.

"You've been in there forever," he said. "What are you doing?"

Joelle frowned. "Throwing up."

He burrowed his eyebrows together. "Oh. That bad, huh?"

"You could say that," she replied, tightly.

"Is there anything I can do?"

"No."

He stuck his face—that handsome face—closer to the crack she'd made in the door. "Are you sure?"

"You can stop worrying," she said. "The baby's fine."

"Yeah—well—good. How about you?"

"Just peachy."

He reached into his shirt pocket and took something out. "How about a peppermint candy?"

A wave of nausea waved across Joelle's stomach. "I don't think so."

"Sure?" he said, giving her a somewhat caring smile.

"I'm sure," she replied.

"Okay. I was just trying to help out."

"Thanks, anyway," she said, giving him a forced smile. "Now I think I'll close the door and finish up in here."

"Yeah, sure," he said, backing up a little. She immediately shut the door.

Finally, after the nausea passed, Joelle began to feel better and was able to pull herself back together. She opened the door to walk out, and much to her surprise, found Gabriel was still standing there, waiting on her.

"Hi," he said, gazing at her curiously. "Are you okay, now?"

"Better," she replied. "I think I'd like to return to my seat, though."

The flight attendant, who was just behind Gabriel gave Joelle a relieved look. "I told him that it was best if he went back to his seat and waited for you there, but he wouldn't listen," she said. Then she smiled. "But, truthfully, it's kind of nice to see a man so concerned about his pregnant wife."

The fact that the flight attendant knew she was pregnant startled Joelle. And, of course, there was only one person who could've told the woman, and right now he was grinning at her as if he'd just won a Golden Globe award for *Best Husband of the Year*.

"I was sort of concerned," he said, as though he had to give her an explanation for being so worried about her. In truth, about the baby. "You stayed in there so long."

She gave him a withering look.

"Come on," he said a second later. "You probably need to sit down." He led them to their seats.

Time passed. Lunch was served and they ate in silence. Mostly Gabriel seemed lost in his own thoughts, and eventually, it became apparent to Joelle that a sort of transformation was taking place in him. It was as though he was deliberately withdrawing himself from her and carefully setting up boundaries for their future relationship. Keeping her own welfare in mind, Joelle reminded herself that he wasn't bringing her home with him because he wanted to. He was doing it because he had to. She was carrying his baby. And it was his baby, and only his baby, that was important to him.

Well, that was just fine with her, she reminded herself. Because he wasn't important to her, either. She was only doing this because it was right for their baby.

During the remainder of the trip, Gabriel found a magazine he liked and kept his eyes glued to what seemed to be one fascinating article after another. In the meantime, Joelle kept herself busy looking out the window at her side.

The pilot came over the intercom and announced that they would soon be landing at the New Orleans airport.

Sitting up straighter in his seat, Gabriel closed the magazine and then ran his fingers down his face as if it was time to wake himself up and face reality. "Uh— look," he said, "I haven't mentioned very much about my housekeeper to you, but I think there's probably a few things you need to know about her."

Turning her head, Joelle looked at him blankly. "Oh?"

"Yeah, well, you see," Gabriel stammered, as though trying to find the right words. That in itself alarmed Joelle. "Her name is Sadie. Some people call her Big Sadie. Anyway, she's been with my family since before I was born, and well, she sort of thinks she rules the roost around my place. And I guess I've never really bothered to tell her differently."

Joelle shrugged. "So... what are you saying?"

"Well," he said, "she can be difficult at times to live with. Overbearing, if you know what I mean. And bossy, too. But she's got a heart of gold."

"Thank goodness," Joelle replied, dryly. "Otherwise, we might think she was perfect."

Gabriel smiled at that.

But Joelle felt like doing anything but laughing. All she needed was a difficult housekeeper to have to contend with.

Just wait until the woman found out that she'd never even been on a farm before. That ought to really sit well with her.

Glancing out the window at her side, Joelle frowned. "I hope she isn't expecting me to be a regular Suzy Homemaker."

"Truthfully, she isn't expecting you at all."

Joelle whipped her gaze around to glare at him. "You mean, you didn't call and tell her I was coming?"

"No."

"And so she doesn't even know about me yet?"

Gabriel shrugged. "She knows you called the house about a month ago."

"Great. She's going to be just thrilled to see me."

Suddenly another thought struck Joelle. "Then she doesn't know about the baby, either."

Gabriel avoided her eyes. "No. Not yet."

"I can't believe this. You're just going to arrive home with me, announce to your housekeeper that I'm your wife and that I'm going to have your baby."

He hesitated momentarily and then said, "Yeah. That's what I'm going to do, all right."

He waited a few moments while Joelle gaped at him and then added, "And just so you'll know what to expect in the next few days, once we've settled in, we're going to get married again. I don't want any problems later on with my baby's birthright."

"Well, of course not," Joelle said, testily. "I mean, isn't that what this whole thing is all about?"

"Exactly," he said. "See, I knew you'd begin to see things my way."

"Frankly," Joelle added dryly, just as their aircraft touched ground, "I don't recall having much of a choice in the matter."

Gabriel leaned in close to her ear and whispered, "You seem to forget, Ames, both of us made our choice the night we climbed in the sack together."

Joelle's blood rushed to her face. "Oh—right—how could I have forgotten that?"

"My thoughts exactly," he replied.

And when Joelle turned to see the expression on his face, she found their mouths were mere inches apart. It almost took her breath away.

Dear God, she thought, but if she was going to survive the coming years, then Mexico was going to have to be a topic of conversation they never discussed. Because even the slightest mention of that time in her life brought back memories of being with him that she knew she had to forget.

She needed to forget.

They were simply too... too wonderful to be a part of the bleak married life she would share with him now.

They both looked away in opposite directions and, once again, fell silent.

Chapter Six

Joelle felt completely out of her element as she gazed out of the window of Gabriel's red pickup truck at the passing scenery. Night had fallen over the area and the flat marshland with its moss-covered cypress trees on both sides of the highway looked hauntingly unfamiliar to her. She was accustomed to sandy beaches, not low terrain filled with murky-looking water and eerie greenery. In truth, given half a chance at the moment, she would've gladly turned around and gone home.

But the engine in Gabriel's truck just kept on humming down the road and she just kept on staring out the window without uttering a sound.

Finally Gabriel turned his pickup off the main road and down a long, narrow driveway lined as far ahead as she could see with huge, sprawling oak trees. Like long, aged fingers reaching out toward the heavens, their moss-laden branches umbrellaed the earth beneath them. Their timeless beauty left Joelle in awe of nature itself and she soon found herself with a new growing respect for Gabriel's home.

Looking ahead, she finally saw the old farmhouse he'd briefly described to her as having been built by his great-great-grandfather. It was a large, white French-Acadian-styled house, complete with an outdoor staircase leading to the attic, which was used at one time for the young boys' room, or as Gabriel explained to her in Cajun dialect, the T-garçons' room. But the daughters of the old Cajun families, he pointed out, always sleep indoors near their parents so that their virtue could be protected. The sons, however, were free to roam.

In some ways, Joelle thought, that standard was still typical of today. Sons always had the advantage. And if anyone questioned that, all they had to do was ask her father what a disappointment having a daughter had been for him.

Finally Gabriel pulled up to the side of the old house and parked near the freestanding double garage set a little ways back from the house. Joelle could tell that that part had been built at a later date. "Well, this is it," he said, gazing out the window as though he was seeing his homestead for the first time in a while. Finally he pushed open the door on his side and stepped to the ground. Drawing in a deep, anxious breath, Joelle did the same. Her legs, however, wobbled beneath her.

"I'll get the luggage," Gabriel said. "It's pretty cold out here. You go on inside. I'll be right behind you."

Truthfully the cool, crisp March winds were a bit too much for her thin cotton long-sleeved shirt. She glanced toward the house and saw someone from inside flick on the porch light. Undoubtedly the helpful person inside was none other than Gabriel's infamous housekeeper. That thought, along with the cold, crisp wind, sent goose bumps splattering over Joelle's skin. Rubbing her arms briskly in the hopes of generating some heat, she said, "I think I'll wait for you."

Gabriel grabbed the luggage from the back of his truck, loading them up under his arms, and then headed for the lighted porch. "Then hurry up and follow me before you end up chilled to the bone," he said.

"I am, already," she replied, falling in step behind him.

"You can't afford to get sick," he said, meaningfully.

"I know," she remarked in a patronizing tone of voice. "Because of the baby." She folded her arms across her middle and shivered.

Gabriel frowned. "You're freezing to death. Come on. Let's get you inside." He quickly got to the door, pushed it open and held it back for Joelle to enter. "Hurry up," he said.

Hugging herself tight, Joelle stepped inside the warm kitchen. Her hands were like icicles. Her feet were numb. But she knew it was probably as much from a case of the nerves as it was from the cold. Still, the warm, cocooned feeling within the room felt extraordinarily good.

"I'll make some hot chocolate," Joelle heard a woman say. She whirled around and saw a stout, average height woman with graying hair get a gallon of milk from the refrigerator and begin pouring it into a pot on the stove. The woman turned on the gas burner beneath it before glancing up at Joelle with what could

PLAY THE "LUCKY 7" SLOT MACHINE GAME!

NO COST! NO OBLIGATION TO BUY!
NO PURCHASE NECESSARY!

PLAY "LUCKY 7"
AND GET FIVE FREE GIFTS!

HOW TO PLAY:

1. With a coin, carefully scratch off the silver box at the right. Then check the claim chart to see what we have for you—FREE BOOKS and a gift—ALL YOURS! ALL FREE!

2. Send back this card and you'll receive brand-new Silhouette Romance™ novels. These books have a cover price of $3.25 each, but they are yours to keep absolutely free.

3. There's no catch. You're under no obligation to buy anything. We charge nothing—ZERO—for your first shipment. And you don't have to make any minimum number of purchases—not even one!

4. The fact is thousands of readers enjoy receiving books by mail from the Silhouette Reader Service™ months before they're available in stores. They like the convenience of home delivery and they love our discount prices!

5. We hope that after receiving your free books you'll want to remain a subscriber. But the choice is yours—to continue or cancel, anytime at all! So why not take us up on our invitation, with no risk of any kind. You'll be glad you did!

This beautiful porcelain box is topped with a lovely bouquet of porcelain flowers, perfect for holding rings, pins or other precious trinkets — and is yours absolutely free when you accept our no risk offer!

NOT ACTUAL SIZE

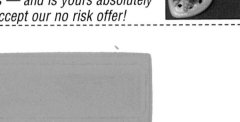

PLAY "LUCKY 7"

Just scratch off the silver box with a coin.
Then check below to see the gifts you get.

YES! I have scratched off the silver box. Please send me all the gifts for which I qualify. I understand I am under no obligation to purchase any books, as explained on the back and on the opposite page.

215 CIS A6NW
(U-SIL-R-01/97)

NAME

ADDRESS _____ APT.

CITY _____ STATE _____ ZIP

7 7 7	**WORTH FOUR FREE BOOKS PLUS A FREE PORCELAIN TRINKET BOX**
🍒 🍒 🍒	**WORTH THREE FREE BOOKS**
⬤ ⬤ ⬤	**WORTH TWO FREE BOOKS**
🔔 🔔 🍒	**WORTH ONE FREE BOOK**

Offer limited to one per household and not valid to current Silhouette Romance™ subscribers. All orders subject to approval.

© 1990 HARLEQUIN ENTERPRISES LIMITED   **PRINTED IN U.S.A.**

only be described as an all-knowing, yet curious expression on her face.

"Hello," Joelle said, her insides trembling with anticipation, regardless of her wish to the contrary. But she did so want to try to make a good impression on this woman. After all, they were going to be living under the same roof. "You must be Sadie. I'm Joelle Ames. I think we spoke over the telephone a few weeks ago."

The older woman scrutinized her for the longest moment, during which Joelle felt this enormous heat rising to her face. She glanced at Gabriel for help, but he didn't appear to be getting ready to offer her any. In fact, he'd opened the refrigerator and was apparently looking for something to eat.

The nerve of him to have an appetite at a time like this. She could've easily boxed him upside the head.

Sadie took a step closer to her. "You're the one from California, ain't you?"

"Uh—yes, ma'am," Joelle said, minding her manners to a tee. Not that she was beginning to think it was going to do her much good. Gabriel's housekeeper reminded Joelle of her father. The older woman looked to have the manner of a drill sergeant. And she, unfortunately, felt like the puny recruit. "Gabriel and I met in Acapulco while we were both on vacation."

"I see," Sadie replied, her mouth forming a hard line.

"Joelle and I were married in Mexico, Sadie," Gabriel said, point-blank. "But the fact is, due to circumstances beyond our control, we're going to have to get married, again, here in the States."

His housekeeper frowned.

Then her eyes widened. "All of this is sort of sudden, ain't it?"

Gabriel shrugged. "Yeah—well, sort of. But there's nothing we can do about that."

"Hmm..." the housekeeper said, first scrutinizing Gabriel, then Joelle. "Seems to me there must be more to this than what's meeting the eye. First, she's calling over here. Then you're going over there. Now, y'all are both here. Somethin's up, all right."

"Well—yeah—there is more," Gabriel said, clearing his throat. "But I'd rather not get into that at the moment. We'll talk about it first thing tomorrow morning. Right now, I'm going upstairs to bring our luggage," he said. Then he shot out the kitchen door toward another part of the house.

"You'd better be right back, Gabe Lafleur," Sadie said to his back in a stern tone of voice. "'Cause you sure enough got some more explaining to do."

Damned Gabriel, anyway, Joelle thought. She was going to get him for leaving her stranded like this with a woman who just might decide to eat her alive.

Left standing alone at the center of the kitchen, Joelle had no earthly idea what to do with herself. Too bad she couldn't simply disappear.

After gazing hard at Joelle for several long moments, Sadie surprised her by motioning toward a chair at one end of the long, wooden dining table and saying, "Sit down, *cher.* You must be tired after such a long day of traveling. The hot chocolate is just about ready and I'm gonna pour you a cup."

Without question, Joelle thanked her and then did as she bid. Besides, a hot cup of anything going down her chilled body sounded pretty good right about now. Probably a stiff drink would've been even better. But she was pregnant, after all. Therefore, even a thimbleful of alcohol was out of the question now.

A moment later, Sadie poured steaming, hot liquid into a mug and placed it in front of her.

Grasping the handle, Joelle blew on the top and then took her first sip.

"Well, how is it?" Sadie asked, still standing next to Joelle.

"Wonderful," Joelle replied. "The perfect end to a harrowing day."

Sadie returned the pot of chocolate to the stove and placed it on the burner that was now turned off. Then, placing her hands on her hips, she faced Joelle. "I'm gonna come straight out with what I've got to say to you."

"Please do," Joelle said, replacing the hot mug on the table, clasping her hands together in her lap and preparing herself for the worst. She wished Gabriel would get himself back downstairs.

"I love Gabe like he was my own son. I don't want to see him get hurt, again. That ex-wife of his almost put him in his grave. It was a blessing when she finally took off." Sadie's dark brown eyes pinned her to the spot. "But, I can tell you right now, I ain't gonna just sit by and let something like that happen to him, again."

"I can understand how you would feel that way," Joelle said. "But, I can assure you, it isn't possible for me to hurt Gabriel in such a way."

Sadie gazed at Joelle meaningfully. "What do you mean?"

"Gabriel and I haven't decided to stick this marriage out because it's what we want. I mean, we're not actually in love, or anything."

Sadie frowned. "Now, that don't make no sense."

"Look, I think I should let Gabriel explain," Joelle replied.

"I see," Sadie replied. "Well, then, in any case, if you're going to be living here, there are a few things I need to know right off. Can you cook?"

Widening her eyes, Joelle shrugged. "Sort of. I make a great tuna salad."

"Tuna salad?" Sadie repeated, dryly. She walked back to where Joelle sat and refilled her mug with hot chocolate. Joelle didn't even think to stop her. She was at a point in her dealings with this woman, that if Gabriel's housekeeper wanted her to drink another mug of hot chocolate, then she would.

Sadie marched back to the stove and replaced the pot on the burner. "Are you accustomed to cleaning your own house?" By now she'd walked back to Joelle and was eyeballing her well-manicured fingernails.

"Uh—I had a maid once a week in San Diego. But, during the week, I kept things up for myself."

"I bet you've never even been to a *boucherie,* much less helped out at one," Sadie replied.

Joelle leaned forward. "I beg your pardon?"

"A butchering," Sadie explained, placing her hands on her hips. "You know, when a hog is slaughtered and fresh cracklins, boudin and hog head cheese are made."

Joelle's stomach rolled over. Twice. She tried swallowing the sudden nausea in her throat. "Good heavens, no," she said. "I could never assist in such a thing. What is all that stuff you just mentioned?"

Sadie shook her head. "My dear child, you've got so much to learn about the goings-on in this part of the country."

Obviously, Joelle thought with a wee bit of anxiety. Undoubtedly Gabriel's housekeeper was out to intimidate her—and, by the way, she was doing a good job of it. "Look," Joelle said, licking her dry lips, "I guess it's pointless of me or Gabriel to put this off any longer. There's something you should know."

"And what's that?" Sadie asked.

"Well—actually—see, Gabriel and I are staying married because... well, because I'm going to have a baby."

There, Joelle thought to herself. She'd finally found the courage to say it.

"A baby," the older woman gasped. "Well, I would have never..." Her voice trailed off as she inhaled a deep breath. Then, slowly, her whole demeanor suddenly changed. Her eyes widened with excitement. "Gabe's baby?" she asked in an awestruck voice.

Unable to speak in that moment, Joelle simply nodded.

"Well, I'll be. Now ain't that somethin'," the old housekeeper replied. "Gabe's going to have his heir, after all."

"Gabriel said that you were going to be thrilled about the baby," Joelle said.

"Why, I sure am," Sadie replied as she wiped her hands on her apron. "This baby is gonna make me as close to being a grandma as I'm ever gonna get."

Joelle smiled tentatively. "Look, Sadie, I'm glad you're pleased. But I'm going to be honest with you. My getting pregnant wasn't exactly something that Gabriel and I planned. We were planning to go our separate ways."

"Is that a fact?" Sadie replied, sounding none too upset over the news. "Well, then I guess the Good Lord has other plans for y'all."

Joelle had no reply for that one. Like Sadie, she believed that God was flawless. It was her and Gabriel's human error she doubted. Still, she wasn't about to argue that point with the housekeeper. "Well, anyway," she finally said, "Gabriel and I have made a deal with each other. We're staying married for the baby's sake, but we plan to continue leading our own separate lives."

The old housekeeper frowned. "Really? Well, let me tell you two somethin', I'm not an old coot for nothing. I've been around a long time. And I can tell you right now. A marriage like that ain't never gonna work out."

Knowing Sadie was probably right, Joelle had enough sense to blush on the inside. She just hoped it didn't show in her face, too.

Sadie gave Joelle a sideward glance. "Then, I guess there ain't no point in me asking you if you love him."

Joelle shook her head. "Love has nothing to do with this. We both feel that we have a responsibility to our child."

Sadie smirked. "Is that a fact?"

Joelle nodded. "It is," she said. Then she sat up erect in her chair. This was one topic she had to get straight with Sadie. Joelle didn't want her, or anyone, for that matter, thinking she was here for any other reason than her baby. It was simply too critical to her own survival that everyone know that she wasn't a clinging, needy woman. Because if there was one thing she knew for sure, if she were to let herself fall in love with Gabriel Lafleur, he would never love her in return.

Suddenly, Sadie marched right up to where Joelle sat. "Look, *cher*, if I'm gonna like you—and I think I already do, then we're gonna have to work together on this."

"Y-you like me?" Joelle asked in awe of the woman's sudden revelation.

"Yeah, I do," Sadie answered, flatly, and then the corners of her mouth barely hinted at a smile. "But now don't go letting it get to your head, okay? And don't go telling nobody, either. People around here think I'm . . . well, that I'm a mean ol' gal, and that's just fine with me."

"But you're not really that, at all, are you?" Joelle replied in a serious tone of voice as a warm, sort of glowing feeling swept through her. Gabriel's ornery old housekeeper had just said she liked her. Joelle took another sip of her hot chocolate. In all due respect, things on the plantation were definitely looking up.

"Now, where's Gabe?" Sadie said as though she already knew the answer. "Ain't no use for him to try and hide out from me. That boy has some explaining to do."

"I'm right here, Sadie," Gabe said, strolling into the kitchen as if nothing was out of the ordinary for him. As if he hadn't just come home with a woman he hardly knew and announced to his world that they were going to get married. "Pardon me if I took a moment too long upstairs. But I had to make a phone call before coming down."

Joelle's heart slammed into her chest. She hadn't asked...she hadn't even thought to ask...but surely, under the circumstances, if he had a girlfriend waiting for him back here, he would've told her so.

He rubbed the back of his neck. "I had to call Blaine," he said as though talking more to his housekeeper than to her, "to make sure he had things ready for planting bright and early tomorrow morning."

"He does," Sadie replied.

Joelle released a deep sigh. Okay, so the truth of the matter was, she knew almost nothing about this man. Therefore, she was bound to jump to the wrong conclusions about him every once in a while.

Her heart continued to pound as he advanced toward the table where she sat. She couldn't help but notice that his jeans fit him snugly—too snug, in fact, for her to draw her eyes away. It was a wonder she hadn't noticed their fit before now. Had she really been that preoccupied?

It was so strange how the events of one night had changed her whole life so completely.

Gabriel pulled out a chair at the kitchen table, sat down and pushed it onto its rear legs. "If it's not too much trouble, Sadie, I'd like a cup of hot chocolate, too."

"Huh," she said, placing a mug in front of him and filling it with hot cocoa. "Looks to me like you've been having more than your share of hot stuff lately."

Joelle almost choked on her swallow of chocolate. The old woman was full of surprises.

Gabriel frowned. "What in the world are you talking about, Sadie?"

"Like you don't know," she replied, dryly.

Gabriel shrugged. "Well, I don't," he said with a laugh.

Sadie just gazed hard at him and smirked.

"Okay, Sadie," Gabriel said, frowning. "Let's have it. What exactly is on your mind?"

Joelle released a deep breath, leaned forward and said right out, "She already knows about the baby. I told her."

"Oh . . ." Gabriel replied, his eyes widening in surprise. He fell silent.

Sadie marched up and peered down at him. "Well, ain't you got nothing to say to that?" she asked.

"Not tonight," he replied, tightly. "I'm tired, and I know Joelle is, too. I don't happen to think it's a good time for discussing anything."

Sadie smirked. "You're probably right. But first thing tomorrow morning, Gabe Lafleur, I'll expect you to come clean with everything. Well," she said wiping her hands on an apron, "it's way past my bedtime. See y'all in the mornin'." With that said, she turned and disappeared through a doorway.

"Well," Gabriel said with a deep sigh, "I'd have to say, Sadie took the news much better than I expected."

"Thank goodness," Joelle replied.

He rose from his chair, scraping the legs against the hardwood floor, and went to the sink with his empty mug. Then he turned to face her. "Are you ready for me to show you to your room?" he asked.

"Uh . . . yes," Joelle stammered. She had no earthly idea why the thought of going to bed—in his house—suddenly had her so rattled. She went to bed every night of her life, for heaven's sake.

He took her mug and placed it in the sink next to his. Then, motioning toward the doorway to his right, he said, "The stairs are this way. Follow me."

Shaken to the core from the prospect of just where her bedroom was going to be in conjunction to his, Joelle stood up from the kitchen table on jellylike legs. The air in the room seemed to decompress. When finally she was able to walk past him, he placed his hand at the small of her back and led her up the stairs. The entire time, Joelle was aware of every single breath he took.

They arrived in a doorway to a bedroom and Joelle saw her luggage on the bed inside. "This will be your room from now on," he said. "Mine's the one across the hall. The bathroom is right next door." He pointed down the hallway to another door. "Just let me know if you need anything."

I might need you.

Ridiculous, she told herself a moment later.

Her hormones were simply overreacting. She was a big girl, after all. Self-sufficient in all the ways that mattered to an independent woman. She didn't need him. She didn't need anyone.

Joelle stepped inside her bedroom and then turned to face Gabriel. "Would it keep you awake if I took a shower right now?"

"Uh..." He ran his long fingers through his dark hair. For some reason, he looked flustered. "No, not at all."

Well, for some reason, she was flustered. Why was this moment so ridiculously awkward?

"Are you sure?" Joelle asked, hesitantly. And then her stomach did a somersault.

"Yeah, I'm sure," he said, his voice suddenly growing hoarse. He cleared his throat. "Like I said," he added, backing up several steps, "just let me know if you need anything."

"Thank you," Joelle said, and to be perfectly truthful, she couldn't wait to close the door to her bedroom. Her insides were tingling with a sudden awareness of him—just like that night in Mexico—and she was hoping that a closed door would somehow shut out the feeling.

"Good night," Joelle said, holding her breath.

Gabe nodded. "Good night."

She immediately closed the door, then leaned her back against it and breathed a sigh of relief.

Then she went to her luggage and chose to remove only those items and clothing she would need for a shower...her nightgown...her robe...a few toiletries...

She opened her bedroom door and tried walking quietly to the bathroom. But as in most old houses, the floor creaked loudly with each step she took. And with each of those steps, Joelle grimaced. When she was only about three feet from her destination, Gabriel's bedroom door opened and he stepped through it, wearing a pair of blue striped pajama bottoms and a white T-shirt. His feet were bare.

Joelle froze. "Were you going to use the bathroom?"

"No," he said, eyeing the items she held in her hands. Her nightgown was on top and it was a sleeveless, straight, slinky, powder pink silk that fell to her midthighs with a lace bodice. Because of her pregnancy, she probably wasn't going to be able to wear it much longer.

In truth, she was probably going to freeze in it tonight. But right now, that was beside the point.

Gabriel's eyes remained on her gown. "Uh...are you wearing that to sleep in, tonight?"

Joelle clutched the items in her hands against her. "Well, yes, I—I was."

"In that case," he said, lifting his eyes to hers and causing her insides to grow warm and shaky, "I'd better make sure you have enough blankets. Even though I've installed central heating, this old house gets pretty drafty at times. But, especially at night." He gave her a slight grin that slid up one side of his face. "You're going to freeze your buns off in that."

"I hope not," she replied, feeling the blood rushing to her face. She felt hot—then cold.

Gabriel motioned toward the bathroom with the tilt of his chin. "You go on and take your shower. I'll check to see if you'll need more blankets on your bed."

Without uttering a sound, Joelle walked into the bathroom and closed the door. She tried the lock, but it was broken. So much for privacy, she thought to herself. She tried the lock again, making sure it wasn't her nerves preventing her from working it properly. It wasn't. The darn thing was broke.

But, of course, she didn't really need to lock herself in. It was just her and Gabriel using the upstairs bath, and Gabriel knew where she was at the moment. He wouldn't dare come in. Tomorrow she would tell him that he needed to change the lock.

Joelle turned on the shower faucets and then opened what she assumed was the linen closet to get herself a towel. Sure enough, the closet was filled with towels, sheets and pillowcases and blankets of all sorts, all folded and stacked neatly in rows. On a bottom shelf were the toiletries such as soap, toothpaste and deodorant. She'd brought her own, though, having packed up everything she could use from her now closed up apartment in San Diego. The rest of her furniture and belongings she had stored until she could decide what she wanted to do with them.

The shower was actually an old claw-foot tub with a shower curtain that encircled it on a flimsy-looking rod. In a bind, the whole setup's lack of stability would've given Joelle reason for concern. But she wasn't in a bind, so she stepped inside and gently pulled the curtain closed, being careful, of course, not to tangle it in any way. The last thing she wanted to do was to destroy Gabriel's shower while using it for the first time.

She heard the light knock but, in all honesty, she thought it was the pipes in the walls that were still clanging from being used. She turned and allowed the water to spill down the back of her head. She was glad she had decided to take a shower before going to bed. It was going to help her relax and make it easier for her to fall asleep.

Suddenly she heard a creak, too, as if a door had opened, but even that didn't alarm Joelle. She lathered up her hair with shampoo and hummed a low tune under her breath just to keep her mind occupied so she wouldn't wonder about Gabriel's whereabouts.

After all, in spite of her vote of confidence in Gabriel's integrity, she hadn't actually been able to forget that the lock on the door to the bathroom didn't work.

Suddenly she heard someone clear his throat. "Uh . . . Joelle, it's just me," Gabriel said.

Well, according to her way of thinking, it being *just him* was enough to constitute a panic. First of all, the clear plastic shower curtain drawn in front of her did little to hide her naked body from his view. Grabbing the curtain with both hands, she yanked it against her. And then, just as she had thought, had she given herself another moment to consider her actions, the entire shower contraption surrounding her came tumbling down. The racket it made was enough to scare away any creature—man or beast—lurking around. Joelle was shocked, no doubt about it.

Stunned, she stood, her mouth gaping, her eyes wide and her hands holding a death grip on the sagging shower curtain. "I—I'm sorry," she stammered.

Gabriel just stared at her in surprise. Eventually he motioned toward the closet with his hand. "I was just going to get a couple of blankets out of here for your bed. I had no idea I would startle you so much." His eyes slowly dropped down the length of her. "Sorry."

Suddenly Joelle's temper ignited. He was sorry? Well, now, wasn't that just great?

Her face pinched together in a frown. She didn't care anymore if she stood half-naked in front of him. By golly, this was his fault, not hers.

She tilted up her chin. "Would you please hand me my robe?"

Her question seemed to pry his eyes from her body and he looked up and in the direction she was pointing to. Grabbing her pink terry-cloth robe, he handed it to her and she slipped it on over her shoulders while he watched. Joelle was very much aware that he had a good view of her breasts while she did so, but with what dignity she could muster, she tied her sash around her waist and looked him square in the face. "This whole setup is a shabby excuse for a shower."

He glowered at her. "Well, this is the first time I've ever had someone pull it down on top of them," he exclaimed.

"Fix the lock," she replied, strutting past him. "Most house guests like privacy."

"Ames?"

She looked up at him. "What?"

"You're not a house guest. You're a permanent resident here, remember?"

Her chin lifted slightly. "Even more reason to replace the broken lock."

He didn't bother to answer her, so Joelle gathered her belongings and marched across the hallway to her bedroom. Once there, she slipped into her nightgown.

There was a knock on her bedroom door. "Ames," Gabriel said in a determined voice, "I'm coming in."

"Well..."

Before Joelle could actually reply, he opened the door and waltzed in. "Here's some more blankets," he said, dumping them on her bed. "It's pretty cold tonight. You're gonna need them."

What she didn't need was for him to keep barging in on her.

Running his fingers through his hair, he glanced her way and frowned.

"What is it?" she asked, a heat unlike anything she'd ever experienced rising to her face. Her breasts tingled with awareness.

Suddenly, pivoting on his heels, Gabriel walked back to the door. Then, turning once again to face her, he dropped his eyes to the lace bodice covering her breasts. A moment later he walked out without saying anything more.

A few minutes later Joelle went to bed, bundling up with the blankets he'd added to her bed, and dreamed of the way it had been for them in Acapulco.

But when she awoke the following morning, she knew without a doubt that their time together for sharing that kind of passion had come and gone.

Besides, it wasn't what she really wanted, anyway. Right?

Chapter Seven

After once again enduring her bout with morning sickness, Joelle dressed in a pair of jeans and a white sweater and went downstairs. Just as she thought, she found Sadie busy at the kitchen sink.

"Good morning," Joelle said.

Sadie turned around and smiled. "Well, it's good to see you up and ready for your first lesson."

Frowning, Joelle slipped the ends of her fingers into the back pocket of her jeans. "My first lesson?"

"That's right," Sadie said with a nod. "In cooking." Her features grew serious. "We don't eat much tuna salad around here."

"Oh," Joelle said, remembering their conversation from the night before. "B-but I thought... Well, I mean, according to Gabriel..."

"You thought I did all the cookin'. Well, I do. But you need to learn, too. Just in case. Never know when the Good Lord is gonna come knocking for Big Sadie. Besides, the more you learn about the running of this here farm, the more you gonna understand and love it the way Gabe and I do, and then the harder it's gonna be for you to ever want to leave and go back to California.''

"Ah," Joelle said, "now I see what this is all about. It won't change anything, Sadie."

Ignoring Joelle's comment Sadie hustled over, took her by the arm and led her to a chair at the kitchen table. "Now, don't you fret. Big Sadie knows what she's doing."

Joelle rolled her eyes. Gabriel was right about his housekeeper. She did think she ruled the roost. She was pushy—too pushy. But what made her so unique was that she was lovable as well. She made you accept her bossiness with a smile.

"Where's Gabriel?"

"Working in the fields. He's been up since before sunrise. We get up early around here."

Joelle grimaced. "I'll try to remember that."

Then she vaguely remembered someone coming into her bedroom and tucking in the covers around her while it was still dark outside. She had thought it had been part of her dream. But, could it have been Gabriel in the flesh, instead?

Well, if it was, she quickly reminded herself, undoubtedly he was just making sure that she was all right for the baby's sake.

Not that she wasn't glad he was concerned about the baby. She was. It was just that sometimes, she wished he was as equally concerned about her. It was childish and selfish to feel that way, but sometimes she did. It seemed that no matter how hard she denied it to herself, there was a part of her that wanted to be loved by a man.

Shake it off, her inner voice told her. It's only because of the unhappy childhood you had growing up under your father's thumb. But you're a grown woman now. You don't need your father—or Gabriel—or any man. You're totally and completely self-reliant.

Without bothering to ask her if she was hungry, Sadie proceeded to fix her a plate of food. She dished out grits, added a stack of pancakes and then poured warm syrup over them. She sat the plate in front of Joelle. "Eat," she said. "You're too skinny."

Joelle couldn't help herself. She smiled. Then she took her first bite and groaned in satisfaction. This was the best tasting breakfast she'd ever had.

Sadie grinned. "That's a girl," she said. Then she turned back to her task at the kitchen sink. "Gabe's gonna be in at noon. He said somethin' about a marriage license and goin' into town. So I guess he's expectin' you to be ready to go with him." Then she turned back to face Joelle. "That's how men are, you know. Women expect babies. Men expect women to know what they're thinkin'. Never occurs to any of them to just say what's on their minds. And, Gabe, God love him, can be one of the worst. He thinks women are mind readers."

Joelle took a swallow of milk and smiled. After wiping her mouth, she said, "To be honest with you, Sadie, I thought you'd be wanting to ask me a lot more questions this morning about—you know—me and Gabriel."

"Nope," Big Sadie said. "Done asked them all of Gabe."

"I see," Joelle replied, placing her glass of milk down on the table. She dropped her hands down into her lap. "Then you understand that this marriage between him and me isn't going to be a traditional one."

"Huh. If you ask me," Sadie replied, "it ain't gonna be nothin', not if the two of you don't open your eyes and see what's just waiting there for both of you."

"Look, Sadie, I know you don't agree with our arrangement."

"Nope, I sure don't," she replied. "But it ain't for me to say. I only work here, remember? Besides, Gabe told me to mind my own business. So I am. My business is cookin' and cleanin' and, when the time comes, helpin' you take care of that young'en of yours. But, in the meantime, I feel it's my duty to teach you everythin' I know about keepin' house. One day you'll thank me for it."

Frowning, Joelle sat back in her chair. If Gabriel thought he'd thawed his housekeeper by telling her to mind her own business, he was in for a big surprise. Joelle didn't know exactly why she felt the way she did, but she had a feeling that Sadie was up to something. But, as far as she was concerned, she couldn't believe she was about to have her first full-fledged lesson in keeping house.

Nonetheless, by ten-thirty that morning, Joelle had had lesson number one in making a chicken potpie. Unfortunately her pie crust in comparison to Sadie's looked as if it had been totally destroyed by an earthquake and then glued back together by a kindergarten class. She had flour all over her clothes, on her face and, probably, in her hair, too. Dried pie crust dough clung to her hands and nails, and all this mess had been accomplished in order for her to have created a pie crust that was, at best, pitiful looking. Heaven help her, but she didn't want to have to eat one single bite of it, and she certainly didn't blame anyone else for feeling the same way. Sadie's pie, however, looked scrumptious.

Sadie slipped both pies into the oven to bake, and then told Joelle that she could wash and dry the dirty dishes while she herself went upstairs to make the beds and clean the bathroom.

Suddenly Joelle remembered the collapsed shower curtain in the upstairs bath. "Oh, Sadie, by the way..."

Sadie stopped in her tracks. "Gabe already told me about what happened to the shower curtain last night." Joelle blushed beet red. "I think he fixed it back up before he went to bed."

"Oh, yeah," Joelle said, now remembering that the shower curtain had been up when she'd gone into the bathroom earlier that morning. How dumb of her to have not given that any serious thought until now. She'd embarrassed herself in front of Sadie for nothing.

Joelle turned back to the chore of getting the kitchen cleaned up before lunchtime, and Sadie went upstairs.

Time passed.

Suddenly the back door swung open and Gabriel came inside wearing a camouflage coat and cap and a pair of work gloves. The first thing he did was remove the gloves from his hands. Then he pulled off his cap and ran his fingers through his hair. His coat came off next and he hung it on a hook by the door.

"Hi," Joelle said, smiling at him.

He took one look at her and started grinning as if he was looking at the funniest thing he'd ever seen.

"What are you grinning about?" she asked, indignantly.

"Come here," he said, taking her by the shoulders and bringing her to where a mirror hung on the wall. "Now, take a look."

One glance and Joelle saw what he was laughing at. She had flour all over her face. "Oh, for heaven's sake," she said, wiping her hands down the sides of her white powdered cheeks, "I look like a clown."

"My thought, exactly," he said, still grinning at her. Glancing at her backside, he began dusting something off her derriere.

As if she needed him to do that.

She didn't dare move, however.

"There," he said after a moment, "at least that side of you is clean now."

The nerve of him to imply she was a mess after all she'd been through in trying to prepare that stupid chicken potpie for his lunch.

"What have you been doing?" he asked.

"Why, playing in flour," she replied in a catty voice and strolled to the kitchen sink. "Isn't that what all newlywed housewives do?"

He grinned and then looked in the flour bowl that hadn't been washed yet. Scooping out a handful of leftover flour, he said, "Like this, you mean," and suddenly threw the handful at her. It hit the center of her chest and then scattered down the front of her clothes.

Dropping her eyes, she gaped at what he'd just done to her. Sucking in a deep breath, she reached inside the flour bowl, came up with a scoop of her own and threw it at him. "No," she said, flatly. "Like this."

Now it was Gabriel's turn to gape at the mess she'd made down the front of his work clothes. Then he glanced back up at her with a devilish gleam in his eyes. "Oh—no, I'm not going to let you get away with this," he drawled in that Cajun accent of his. And then suddenly he was holding up another handful of flour to throw at her.

"You started it," Joelle squealed, just about the time she received her second blow of flour down the front of her. Only this time, some of it landed in her hair and face.

"Oh..." she moaned, blinking twice. She glanced around in disgust of the mess *he* was making all over the kitchen she'd worked so hard to clean. She'd show him. Grabbing the flour bowl, she stood on her tiptoes and dumped what was left in it over his head. It tumbled down on his head as if it were a fine powdered rain.

Without moving a muscle he batted his eyes several times. Then, suddenly, with a mischievous grin on his face, he reached out and pulled her against him. It was hard and fast—and without the slightest warning. It was like *slam-bam*—and then she was pressed against his hard, powerful body. A sensual awareness of his maleness stung to life every cell in her body.

Her eyes widened. "What do you think you're doing?"

His grin slipped to one side of his face. "What I should've done the moment I walked in here." And then he did the one thing she told herself he wouldn't dare do. He kissed her, damn him. Hard.

Finally he released her and looked toward the doorway behind her. After regaining her wits, Joelle glanced back over her shoulder and saw Sadie standing there, grinning at them.

"Oh, Sadie," Joelle said, springing away from Gabriel in one quick move. She wiped her hands down the sides of her jeans. Her lips still tingled from his kiss. "I'm sorry about the mess in your kitchen."

Sadie shrugged and then began shaking her head. "It don't bother me none that y'all two was actin' like children. Y'all done made the mess, now y'all can clean it up."

"Oh, we will," Joelle said with a promise in her voice. "Right this very minute."

Sadie grinned as if she was actually enjoying herself. "Good. You make sure that Gabe helps you, too."

Joelle blushed.

Gabriel cleared his throat. "We were just fooling around," he said.

"Huh," Sadie said. "Well, it seems to me that that's what's got the two of you in this mess in the first place." And then she turned and headed back upstairs.

Looking at Joelle, Gabriel renewed his grin. "You look a sight."

She grinned back at him. "So do you."

A moment later, they both laughed.

And then suddenly, they grew serious and the tension that seemed to underline their relationship these past few days returned.

"You shouldn't have kissed me like that," she said.

"And you shouldn't have let me," he replied.

Joelle gaped at him indignantly. "Like I seemed to have had any choice in the matter."

"Well, I damned sure didn't force you."

"No, you didn't," she replied. "But... Just don't do it again, okay?"

He leaned forward, closer to her face. Their mouths were mere inches apart. "Okay, I won't." And then he straightened up. "Now, let's get this mess cleaned up. It's almost lunch and I'm starving."

Joelle thought about the pies in the oven and sucked in a deep breath. She ran to the stove and opened the oven door. But nothing was smoking, thank goodness. In fact, the two pies, as pathetic-looking as one of them was, seemed to be browned just enough. She took Sadie's pie out first, then the one that she'd made.

Gabriel came up behind her. "Who made that one?" he said.

"I did," she replied.

"Oh."

She turned to him with a bright smile on her face. "Want a slice?"

"Uh..."

Joelle knew she had him cornered now and was loving it. "Well... do you or don't you want to sample the pie I made?"

He rubbed his head as though stalling for time. Well, she wasn't going to give him time to find an excuse for saying no.

"Here, sit down," she said. "I'll cut you a piece." With that said, she cut a huge slice from the pie she'd made. She, however, planned to eat Sadie's.

"Aren't you eating?" he asked when she handed him his plate. She almost grinned at the sick-looking expression on his face.

"No, I'm going to clean up the kitchen first."

"I'll help," he said, starting to rise.

"Oh, no, that's all right," she said, placing her hand on his shoulder. "I wouldn't want your slice to get cold. I'll clean the kitchen by myself. You sit down and enjoy your food."

"How thoughtful of you," he said dryly, eyeing the piece she'd served him.

Joelle ignored him and began wiping the countertop. But from the corner of her eye, she watched as he took his first bite. She watched as his chewing slowed and then his features pulled together in a frown.

She walked up in front of him and smiled. "Well, how does it taste?" she said, barely able to contain her laughter.

He continued to chew with an odd look on his face. "I'm not sure," he finally replied.

"Well, Sadie said that I had to add corn starch as a thickening agent, but, you know, I think I added salt instead. What do you think? Is it a bit too salty?"

Finally he swallowed. "Just a bit," he replied in a kind of hoarse-sounding voice. "Could I have a glass of water?"

"Certainly," Joelle said in a cordial tone of voice. She went to the kitchen sink and filled a glassful. "Ice?" she asked, glancing back at him from over her shoulder.

He shook his head. "Just water," he said.

She handed him the glass and he drank it.

"More?" she asked.

He put his hands out in front of him. "No, that one bite filled me up. Thanks, anyway."

"I was talking about the water," Joelle replied, pretending to suffer from a moment of indignation. And to be perfectly honest, in some ways, her pride was hurt. What did he expect from her after only one lesson? Suzy Homemaker, extraordinaire? She never claimed to be domesticated, not by any measure. Her expertise was in other areas. She was a damned good advertising representative.

Gabriel wiped his hands with his napkin and then sat back in his chair. "Have you gained any weight— I mean, since you've been pregnant. You don't look like you have. You seem to be the same size you were in Acapulco."

The fact that he was observing her so closely rattled Joelle. She splayed her hands across her abdomen. "Maybe a couple of pounds."

"Well, you don't want to gain too much."

"I know," she said, sighing deeply. "It isn't good for the baby."

"Well, it isn't good for you, either, from what I understand."

"What do you care, how it affects me?" Joelle asked.

"Hey, it's your body. I was just asking a question, okay?"

"Well, then don't worry about my body. I can take care of myself."

He immediately stood up from his chair. "Well, now, that certainly takes a load off my mind." Then, before walking away, he turned and said, "I'm going upstairs to take a shower. When I'm done, I'll be ready to leave for town."

Joelle glanced down at her flour-covered clothing. "I think I'll go like this," she said, defiantly. She knew she was going to get a reaction from him. In fact, she was hoping for one.

"Suit yourself. The personnel in the clerk of court's office will probably think I'm getting ready to marry a nut, but who cares?" he said, rushing up the stairs two at a time.

Joelle followed him to the foot of the stairs. "I am a nut for letting you talk me into coming here," she yelled up at him.

He stopped at the top of the stairwell. "Well, it's too late now to change your mind."

"Like hell it is. I can walk out of here anytime I want." *Only she didn't want,* she suddenly realized.

He came back halfway down the stairs, placed his hands on his hips and glowered at her. "If you weren't having my baby, maybe you could. But it's too late to even consider such a thing now. The truth of the matter is, as soon as we met in Mexico, our fate as man and wife was sealed. We just didn't know it, yet."

Joelle placed her hands on her hips. "You know something, Lafleur, you really have a way of making things sound so romantic."

His eyes narrowed. "If you're looking for romance, then go rent yourself a video. Better yet, buy yourself a book."

"You know, I think I'll do just that," Joelle replied, sarcastically, her hands on her hips. "At least the jerks in them sometimes turn out to be nice guys, after all. That's more than I can say for you."

"Just be ready to leave in fifteen minutes," he said through clinched teeth.

"I'm ready now," she replied, heatedly, giving him a plastic smile.

He simply grunted on that remark, turned and stormed up the stairs.

Joelle turned and found Sadie standing right behind her. Shaking her head, Sadie placed her hands on her hips and said, "Land's sakes, sure sounds to me like the two of you are falling in love, all right."

Joelle frowned. "That's ridiculous, Sadie. Who could possibly fall in love with an arrogant man like that?" A few moments later she and Sadie heard a door slam upstairs and Joelle assumed that Gabriel had entered the bathroom for his shower. Sadie walked off shaking her head from side to side. Joelle inhaled deeply and marched back into the kitchen to clean up the mess she and Gabriel had made. Minutes later she rushed up to her bedroom and changed out of her flour-ladened clothing. It took her but a moment to clean her face and brush flour clumps from her hair. Then she slipped into a black denim jumper and raced back down the stairs in the hopes of arriving at the door before Gabriel. But he was waiting for her when she got there.

He smirked and then allowed his eyes to drop down the length of her. "You clean up nicely," he said.

"I'm not talking to you."

"That's fine with me," he replied.

He opened the back door and she pranced out ahead of him as if she was in total control of herself. But, of course, she wasn't. In fact, she had begun to notice that when she was around Gabriel, her internal motor seemed to be running on high. They strolled to his truck without uttering a sound and climbed inside. In no time at all, it seemed, they were heading in the direction of the parish courthouse.

Finally, Gabe said, "Did you remember to bring along some identification—like your birth certificate, for example."

"I have everything I need in my purse," she replied, tightly.

"Good. Because I know a few people who work at the courthouse. I would hate for them to think that we don't know what we're doing."

"Well, at least they'd be right," she replied.

Getting a marriage license was easy. It took them less than thirty minutes from the time he parked his truck, until the time they climbed back into the cab with their marriage license in tow.

Gabriel drove off in a different direction. Joelle was curious as to where they were heading, but she wasn't about to ask him. Instead she sat on the passenger side and pretended not to care.

Several red lights and two right turns later he pulled into the parking lot of a shop with a sign out front that said Baby's Merry-Go-Round. He killed the engine to his truck, opened his door and said, "Let's get down."

Without hesitation, Joelle got out of the truck. Gabriel waited for her to catch up with him. "I knew this place was here because I do a lot of business with that hardware store across the street."

Joelle glanced back.

"I see," she said, using her hand to block the sun from her eyes. "What are we doing here?"

He pulled the cap he was wearing lower over his eyes to shade them from the glare. "Well, since we were in town, I figured we'd just as soon do some shopping for the baby."

"Already," she said, flabbergasted. Never in her wildest dreams had she expected them to be shopping for baby items so soon.

But, obviously, he was ready. But, then again, the baby was all he seemed to care about. She cared, too, but...

"Come on," he said, taking her by the hand. "Let's go inside."

The shop was jam-packed with baby items, from clothing and toys to furniture. The saleslady was pleasant and was delighted to help them make their selections.

Soon it was apparent to Joelle, and the saleslady as well, that Gabriel had come for the sole purpose of furnishing a complete nursery. Joelle chose a Jenny Lind baby bed with matching crib, a chest of drawers and a dressing table. Gabriel picked out a soft brown teddy bear and a carousel night-light to go on top of the chest of drawers. The saleslady piled on comforters, sheets, waterproof pads and receiving blankets. She showed Joelle their stock in christening attire, but then Gabriel said he still had the white christening outfit that his mother had made for him and would like very much for his child to wear it. Joelle thought it a wonderful idea.

Joelle went from one aisle to another looking over the lovely display of merchandise. Suddenly her gaze fell on a beautiful white blanket that had been embroidered at the corners. "This is so lovely," she said, touching it.

Gabriel strolled over to where she stood with a strange, sort of mellow expression on his face. "What is it?" he asked, his voice sounding deep in his throat.

"Just a blanket," she said. "But it's wonderful the way it's been embroidered." Joelle looked up at the saleslady. "How much is it?"

"I'm not sure. It's handmade, so I know it's more than some of the ones we order through our manufacturer."

"We'll take it, anyway," Gabriel said, practically lifting the box the blanket came in from Joelle's hands.

Surprised, Joelle glanced up at him. "Maybe we ought to wait for the price," she said.

"You like it, don't you?" he replied, gazing down at her.

Joelle suddenly realized that they were standing very close together and her heart began to pound. "Y-yes," she replied. "But—"

"Look, it's only a baby blanket. It can't be that much."

Gabriel handed the box to the saleslady and she took it to the checkout counter. He glanced at Joelle and said, "Oh, by the way, did I tell you that I've gotten the name of an obstetrician for you?"

Joelle gaped at him. "You've really been busy making all kinds of plans, haven't you?"

"This baby is important to me."

"Well, it just so happens, this baby is important to me, too."

"I know that," he replied.

"Sometimes, I wonder," Joelle said.

A few moments later, Gabriel paid for their purchases, loaded up what he could in the back of his pickup and then made an appointment with the saleslady for a delivery truck from the shop to bring the larger items out to his plantation the following afternoon.

After that, Gabriel drove home and then went back to work in the fields. Sadie was busy with several household chores. Joelle went upstairs and began cleaning out the bedroom that was going to be the baby's nursery. When Gabriel came in that night, he stepped inside the room momentarily while on his way to take a shower. He looked around, seemingly approved of what she was doing and walked out.

Sadie served the chicken potpie for supper—hers, not Joelle's. Obviously she'd sampled Joelle's at some point during the day and had thrown the suffering thing away. Eventually idle conversation sprang up among the three of them, and Gabriel said that according to the *Farmer's Almanac,* this year's winter cold was going to linger on for a few more weeks. He wasn't at all pleased about that. After supper he went into his study, and Joelle helped Sadie in the kitchen. The older woman never once mentioned the failure of Joelle's cooking lesson that day. Once the supper dishes were done, Sadie said good-night and then retired to her bedroom.

Joelle knocked on the door to Gabriel's study.

"Come in," he said.

She opened the door and stepped inside. The fireplace was ablaze, and it made the room feel cozy and warm. Gabriel sat in a large platform rocker with his feet stretched out on a hassock facing it. "I hope I'm not interrupting," she said, cautiously.

He looked up, then folded the newspaper he was reading and laid it down in his lap. "That's all right," he said. "Have a seat."

She did.

He sat silently, waiting, she knew, for her to say what was on her mind. "I—uh—I was just wondering," she said, "what do you do around here at night for entertainment?"

His brown eyes suddenly twinkled. "That depends. Just what did you have in mind?"

She wasn't about to take the bait on that one. Her question was a legitimate one, and he had some nerve implying otherwise. She cleared her throat. "What I mean is, do you ever drive into town for a movie?"

He shook his head. "Not often. Not at this time of year, anyway. I'm usually too tired at night to do much of anything. In fact, I usually go to bed early."

"Oh."

He studied her for the longest moment and then reached toward the table next to him and picked up a remote control. A moment later, he clicked on the big screen television that was in one corner of the room.

Pleased to have something to occupy her idle time for tonight, Joelle crossed her arms over her chest and turned in her seat so that she would have a better view of the TV screen. She didn't care what program was on.

"I'm probably going to doze off," she said. "I usually do when I watch TV in a reclining position."

"Be my guest," he answered. Joelle heard when he picked up the newspaper, again. She smiled to herself. It felt so cozy in here.

And then she proved herself right. Within fifteen minutes, she was having extreme difficulty keeping her eyes open. But she wasn't totally asleep, yet, when she felt someone covering her with a blanket. Her eyes opened momentarily and she saw Gabe standing over her. "Thank you," she mumbled, closing her eyes once again.

And then she could've sworn that someone actually tucked that blanket in around her and kissed her on the forehead. But she was so out of it by then that she figured it had to have been a dream.

Gabe stood over Joelle and watched her momentarily before finally dropping back down into his chair. Still, he continued to look at her... to study her... to wonder what it was about this woman that fascinated him. Fascinated him so much, in fact, that he'd actually lost his head and wanted to marry her in Mexico for no reason at all.

She still fascinated him... drawing him to her against his will in a way no woman had ever done before. Not even his ex-wife. And as much as he hated to admit it, there was a part of him that was glad she was having his baby. It was crazy, he knew, but it was true. A part of him wanted her near him. Like now. In fact, he was getting a whole lot of pleasure from just watching her sleep. It was ridiculous of him, and he had absolutely no reason for feeling that way, but he did.

In truth, he didn't really need a reason for his feelings.

Joelle Ames *was* important to him, but only because she was going to have his baby. End of discussion.

She moved slightly, and his heart jumped ahead several beats. She wasn't his type, though, even if she did have the poutiest, sexiest-looking mouth he'd ever seen on a woman. The fact that he wanted to carry her up to his bedroom right now and make love to her as he had in Mexico was purely hormonal. She was all woman, after all, and his libido had always run high.

Gabe sat back in silence, his elbows resting on the armchair, his hands folded and thoughtlessly placed under his chin, and watched her every breath until the flames in the fireplace died down to embers, at which time the study began to grow chilly. Making as little noise as possible, he rose from his chair, lifted her into his arms and carried her upstairs to bed. By the time he'd gotten to the middle of the hallway separating their bedrooms, his desire for her soared even higher, making his need to have her seem almost impossible to resist.

But, finally, he took a deep, steadying breath and pulled himself together. And after tucking her into her own bed for the night, he closed the door to her room and walked across the hall to his.

But as he crawled in under the cold, crispy sheets, he told himself that this was the last time that he was going to be so foolishly chivalrous. The next time Joelle invaded his privacy, only to fall asleep on his sofa—practically in his arms—she had better damned well not take it for granted that she was going to wake up in her own bed the following morning.

Deal, or no deal, he was tired of her flaunting that sexy little body of hers in front of him. Besides, over the past two months, he had regained most of his memory of their night together in Mexico. And he knew exactly what he was missing out on.

Chapter Eight

Joelle and Gabriel were married three days later in a simple ceremony at city hall. Afterward, Gabriel drove them home and for supper that night they ate the shrimp and okra gumbo Sadie prepared. When it was time to retire to bed, they each went into their bedrooms and closed their doors behind them as though nothing out of the ordinary had taken place that day.

Since the morning after Joelle had fallen asleep in Gabriel's study, she had awakened to find that he was now even more aloof toward her than ever before. She had no earthly idea why—other than the fact that he'd obviously felt it his duty to carry her upstairs and put her to bed in her clothes that night—which, of course, was ridiculous of him to have thought so. But, regardless of his reasons for being even more distant with her now, she had decided not to let it bother her. Needless to say, however, he never invited her to join him in his study after supper, and she never took it

upon herself to do so, again. In fact, they were leading separate lives now, exactly as they had agreed to.
Oh, there was that one time when he helped her to ar-
range the new furniture in the baby's nursery. He'd
seemed excited about that for the few hours it had
taken them. But other than that one time, he was distant. Her appointment with her new obstetrician was
in two days, and she wondered if he was still planning
to take off long enough from planting his cane fields
to go along with her. A part of her wanted him there
with her, but another part of her was very upset because she felt that way.

One thing was for sure. With nothing much to keep
her occupied during the day and no one to talk to at
night, she was getting lonely. Thank goodness for Sadie. Joelle was grateful for the older woman's friendship—and her guidance. In truth, Big Sadie was
becoming the mother figure she had never known.

For the most part, Gabriel was so wrapped up in his
own world of work, come home, go to bed and then
back to work the following morning, again, that he
hardly seemed to notice the growing friendship between them. One morning, though, as she was quietly
descending the stairs, she heard Sadie getting on his
case because of his attitude toward her. But, the last
thing Joelle wanted was to come between the two of
them, so she asked Sadie not to champion her cause
with him, anymore.

"I'm fine, Sadie," she said. "Really I am. There's
no need for you to stay after Gabriel on my account."

Sadie only shook her head as she walked away.
"That man had better wake up before it's too late and
you and that baby of his is done gone back to California."

"I made a deal with him," Joelle said, reminding Gabriel's housekeeper of that fact. "I promised that I would stay here in Louisiana so we could raise our child together. No matter what, I plan to honor it."

Suddenly turning, Sadie looked at her with the saddest eyes. "You know, *cher,* I'd hate to see you leave. I'd miss you terribly. And God knows, I never thought I'd see the day when I'd say somethin' like this to a wife of Gabe's. But, sometimes, a woman can take only so much and then she's got to do what she's got to do."

Joelle frowned. "I won't leave here, Sadie. No matter what."

Sadie smiled sadly. "I know it's not something you're planning to do."

Joelle dropped her eyes to the floor momentarily before glancing back up. "Sadie, may I ask you a question?"

"Now, you know that you can ask me anythin' you'd like."

Joelle took in a slow, deep breath and then released it. "Was Gabriel distant like this with his first wife?"

Immediately Joelle could tell that her question stunned Sadie because the old housekeeper's eyes widened. But then a moment later she frowned. "No. In fact, he was just the opposite. He lavished that woman with attention and gifts and she didn't appreciate one bit of it."

"Oh," Joelle replied, her heart sinking somewhat. So, her intuition was right, after all. Gabriel's attitude toward her was an isolated case and not because it was his nature to be distant. In some ways, she'd known that all along. So, okay, she was a big girl. She could live with it. Right?

Right.

Sadie pulled her eyebrows together. "Sometimes I think that's why he's so distant now. He's afraid of being hurt, again." Then she sighed heavily. "Well, I guess it's time I get supper started."

"I think I'll go for a walk outside," Joelle replied.

Gabriel strolled in that night, showered and then came back downstairs for supper dressed in a blue flannel shirt and a pair of old worn-out jeans. He surprised both Joelle and Sadie when he suddenly came around and pulled out Joelle's chair for her to sit in at the table. Stunned, Joelle could barely mumble a thank-you as she sat down. A few moments later, Sadie announced she wasn't hungry and quickly disappeared into another part of the house. After she was gone, Gabriel actually attempted to carry on a conversation with her by asking what she'd done that day. Needless to say, she was able to account for her rather boring day in one short paragraph. But, even more surprisingly to Joelle, when she asked him about his day, he opened up and gave her a detailed report, right down to the three-hour delay he'd had because one of his tractors had broken down. When they were done, he helped her clear away the table and put the dishes into the dishwasher.

As much as Joelle hated to admit it, having this time to share with him was heaven. She was starving for his attention, just as she'd once starved for her father's. In fact, she hated to see the moment end. She didn't know if Sadie had actually done so intentionally, but she was grateful, nonetheless, for the older woman's insight in leaving them alone at the kitchen table.

"Would you care to join me in the study?" he asked, just as Joelle was thinking it was time for her to go upstairs to her bedroom and be lonely, again.

"Uh—I—uh—I suppose so," she replied, her heart pounding. That was the last thing she was expecting him to ask her. First, there had been a decent conversation with him at the supper table and now this. It was almost too good to be true. Surely someone was going to pinch her awake soon. "Is there anything worth watching on television tonight?"

"Why would you care?" he said, grinning at her. Her stomach went *k-plunk*. This sudden change in his attitude had her head spinning. "You'll probably fall asleep, anyway," he added, his eyes suddenly twinkling with amusement.

Joelle's heart continued to pound.

In spite of herself, she grinned back at him and shrugged. "Yeah, you're right," she said. "I usually do."

They went inside the study and Gabriel closed the door. Then he strolled to the fireplace and lit a stack of logs. Joelle sat down on the sofa in the same place she had the one and only other time she'd ever joined him in the room after supper. After making sure the logs in the hearth were going to stay lit, Gabe brushed off his hands and then sat down in his chair. Soon the flames from the fire he'd started were flickering brightly. Eventually they began to crackle and pop, and the room started to glow with a shadowy warmth.

Stretching out his long, muscular legs in front of him, Gabriel rested his feet on the hassock. Joelle was expecting him to turn on the TV at this point, but he didn't. Instead he began watching her in a silent, unnerving manner.

"Aren't you going to turn on the television?" she finally asked, crossing her legs and then recrossing them. She hated the feeling that she was being put on center stage.

"In a minute," he replied, lazily, as though answering her question hadn't even interrupted his deep concentration. To add proof to that fact, his eyes never wavered from her face. But then a moment later, he said, "I just wanted to mention that I've taken time off from work to take you to your doctor's appointment on Wednesday."

So he hadn't forgotten about that. Well, at least now she knew what this meeting was all about. And it had nothing whatsoever to do with him wanting her company for the evening. Her heart sank.

He cleared his throat. "And, uh, there's something else," he said. "I just happened to notice your jeans tonight."

"My jeans?" she replied, incredulously. "What about my jeans?"

"They're getting tight. We probably need to take you shopping for some new clothes."

Joelle gazed at him indignantly. "We?"

He gave a short laugh. "Look, all I meant by that was, after your doctor's appointment, maybe I could take you shopping for some bigger clothes."

"Bigger," she repeated. "Are you insinuating that I'm getting fat?"

He frowned. "Look, Ames—I mean, Joelle— you're taking this all wrong."

She crisscrossed her arms at her waist. "Oh—really?"

"Yes, really," he said. "Look, all I meant was, it's probably time that you start wearing more loose-fitting clothes. You know, the kind that stretches as your stomach grows."

After giving her husband a heated look, Joelle finally glanced down, placed her hands on her stomach and sighed heavily. "Yeah, Lafleur, I guess you're right. My stomach is definitely growing."

"With my baby," he said, his voice suddenly sounding hoarse.

With pulses racing, Joelle glanced up and her gaze locked with his. She could hardly breathe. "Yes," she finally whispered, "with your baby."

"I like that," he said.

"You do," she replied.

"Yeah. I like it just fine."

"Oh."

Finally, after several tension-filled moments, he leaned back in his chair and released a deep breath. "Anyway, I just thought I'd let you know that I don't mind taking you shopping."

Joelle nodded in awe. "Thank you."

"Good," he replied, giving her a fleeting smile. A second later he reached for the remote control and clicked on the television.

Realizing their conversation from a moment ago was now ended—though, surprisingly, this time on a good note—Joelle turned, lounged back against the arm of the sofa with a throw pillow under her head and began to watch TV.

And as normal, it wasn't too long after that when she found her eyelids growing heavy. She fleetingly thought of getting up and going to bed, but it was so comfortable where she was by the fire. So cozy... Besides, Gabriel was sitting so near...

Finally, without even realizing it, she gave up the fight altogether and fell sound asleep.

Gabriel sat there in his chair, gazing at her. Dammit, he'd tried his best to stay away from her. He'd told himself that, if he worked hard enough in his cane fields from sunup to sundown, seven days a week, he would eventually be able to rid himself of this deep down yearning he had for her. But he had been mistaken. Badly mistaken. His efforts hadn't worked. If anything, they'd backfired. Actually the only thing he had gotten so far for all his trouble was Sadie's wrath. As far as his need for Joelle was concerned, it was still very much alive and well. Thriving, even. In fact, from the time she'd walked into the kitchen tonight in those jeans of hers that were a tad bit too tight for him not to have noticed their fit, he'd begun to plan in the back of his mind exactly what he was going to do.

And now he'd done it. She had fallen asleep on his sofa and was vulnerable, and all his for the taking.

Not that he planned on making love to a sleeping woman. He wasn't that low—or desperate. But he did plan to bring her to his bed and allow her to awaken there in the morning. Then, after breakfast, he'd tell Sadie to move his wife's belongings across the hall to his bedroom. That ought to delight his housekeeper. God knew, she'd been champing at the bit to have him and Joelle sleeping in the same bed together since the day they'd gotten married.

But, as far as Joelle was concerned, he knew he couldn't let himself get in too big a hurry to make her his. He'd only mess things up with her if he did. Therefore, after her initial move into his bedroom, he planned on taking it one day at a time until he got what he wanted—needed—from her. They were husband and wife, after all. According to the way he now saw things, it was a natural progression in their relationship. After all, why not share a great sex life while passing away all those years together? It sure sounded like a damned good idea to him.

Gabe lifted Joelle into his arms and she only groaned once in her sleep at being moved. But, halfway up the stairs, she suddenly slipped her arm around his neck, and he almost lost control of his better judgment right then and there. Almost. Damn her, anyway, for making life so difficult for him.

He continued up the stairs to his bedroom where he placed her down on his side of the mattress. Then, after throwing back the covers on what was going to be her side of the bed, he placed her there and then removed her jeans so she could sleep more comfortably. She actually lifted her hips to help him accomplish that task. He grew hard at the sight of her smooth legs. He wished those legs of hers were wrapped around him. Actually he wanted to rip off every single stitch of her clothing and view her naked as he had done in Mexico. And, one of these days, he would. But, for now, he couldn't allow himself to move that fast. As it was, Joelle was undoubtedly going to be shocked out of her mind when she woke up in the morning and found that she'd spent the night in his bed.

With a heat in his loins to match that of the smoldering embers in the fireplace downstairs, Gabe removed all his clothing, down to the bare skin, and slipped in under the covers next to her.

He wanted her, moved in and pulled her against him.

She felt good.

He was hard. Hot.

And growing more so by the minute.

But he owed her something. Respect, he supposed. She was his wife. The mother of his unborn child.

He would wait.

Yes, he told himself, again. He would.

With that somewhat resentful decision behind him, Gabe banked his libido in a place inside him that he hoped was as secure as a federal reserve bank. Then he slipped his arm over her waistline and, eventually, fell into a deep, restful sleep.

When he awoke early the next morning before sunup, he found that Joelle was still snug against him, only they had switched positions at some point during the night. Now his back was to her and her arm was thrown around his waist.

And he was on fire—hot, hard—and in need of release so badly that he feared the slightest move from her just might be his undoing.

She groaned and then pressed herself against him, but he lay motionless, wanting to keep himself in control. But, then, suddenly, her hand began to slide down toward his groin area and a moment later she found him.

He groaned. She stroked.

And then he couldn't take any more. Dammit, he'd tried his best, but this was too much. He rolled over and pinned her beneath him. "Joelle," he said, his voice gravelly with desire. His hands came up to each side of her head. "I want you."

Without opening her eyes to look at him, she smiled and then tilted up her face so that her lips became her most dominate feature to him. "Kiss me," she said.

And, so, he did. Passionately, relentlessly, with all the fire and need and longing pent up in his soul. And she responded with equal vigor, moaning and groaning and leading him to believe she didn't want him to stop—ever.

And, so, he didn't. Instead he took her along with him and gave her what he felt she wanted—what he knew he wanted to give her more than anything else in that moment. Joelle abandoned herself to him, and when at last daylight finally crept in over the earth, they lay, side by side, sated. They knew in the silence of their hearts that they had just shared something very special. Something much more than just sex. Their need for each other had been raw—needy— desperate. But, of course, neither one of them was willing to admit that now that the moment had passed. Not even to themselves.

Suddenly Sadie was knocking on the door to Gabriel's bedroom and asking, "Gabe, are you in there? Why ain't you up, yet? It's past time."

Gabe cleared his throat. "I'll be down in a minute, Sadie. I just overslept."

"Huh, that's odd," she mumbled. They could hear the floor creaking under her weight as she shuffled away.

Gabe knew he needed to get out of bed and get to work, but, still, he didn't move from Joelle's side.

Finally, lying flat on her back, Joelle said, "Why did you bring me in here last night? Why not to my own bed?"

Gabriel continued to stare at the ceiling overhead. "I don't know. I just decided to bring you in here."

"We had a deal, and this wasn't part of it."

"We still have a deal. It's just been modified to fit the way our relationship has changed. It was inevitable. I knew that—and so did you."

"That's bull," Joelle said.

"Hey, look, I didn't hear you objecting to what we just did together. In fact, I'd have to say, it was quite the contrary."

"What did you expect?" she replied, finally turning her head so she could glare at him. "It isn't every day that I wake up and find myself in bed with a naked man."

"You could've gotten up," Gabriel replied. "I wouldn't have stopped you."

"This was a setup and you know it."

"You're right," he said. "But, you know what?" Gabe continued, suddenly throwing back the covers from his nude body and climbing out of bed, "I don't have any regrets. We have a long life together ahead of us. Why not enjoy some of it?"

Joelle visibly paled. "I can't believe you have the nerve to say something like that!" she exclaimed.

Naked as the day he was born, Gabe marched around to her side of the bed and placed his hands on his hips. "And why not? We're married."

Joelle could only gape at him...at his nakedness...his manhood that had just given her so much pleasure... She swallowed.

A moment later, he turned away from her and began dressing. "Look, when I go downstairs, I'm going to tell Sadie to help you get your things moved in here today. We're man and wife. From now on, we sleep together."

Just like that, Joelle thought, and according to Gabriel, it was a done deal. No fanfare. No three little words that would've made all the difference in the world to her.

He finished getting his clothes on, marched to the door to leave and then gave her one last glance back from over his shoulder. "I'll see you tonight," he said. A moment later, he was out the bedroom door, closing it behind him.

It took Joelle quite a while to gather up her courage and go downstairs to face Sadie. Not that she didn't think Sadie was going to approve of her moving into Gabriel's bedroom. Joelle knew better than that. She knew, more than anything, Sadie wanted for her and Gabriel to find a peaceful, common ground between them. But the old housekeeper had no way of knowing that Gabriel had but one reason for wanting his wife in his bed. He wanted her for sex.

Well, as much as she hated to admit it, and in spite of herself, Joelle now realized that she'd fallen hopelessly in love with her husband—the man who had fathered her child. She needed a lot more from him than sex. But, for now, at least, she'd take what she could get and hope that love would follow someday. As long as she could hang on to even a fragment of hope, she'd be all right.

Sadie was singing to herself in Cajun French when Joelle finally came downstairs. She immediately assured Joelle that the decision to move her things across the hall to Gabriel's room was for the best.

"It wasn't my idea," Joelle stated.

"It don't matter," Sadie said, happily. "It's happened and that's all that counts."

"But you don't understand," Joelle began.

"I do, too," Sadie said, giving her a long, hard look. "So I hope you ain't gonna try to tell me that you don't love my Gabe," she said.

Joelle took a deep breath and then sighed. "No, I'm not going to tell you that, because you already know me too well. But this is one time you're wrong about Gabriel. He doesn't love me."

"He might not know it, yet, but he loves you," Sadie replied, steadily.

"I'm telling you, Sadie. He simply thinks that since we're married, we ought to share the benefits that go along with it, if you know what I mean."

"I wasn't born yesterday, *cher*. I know exactly what you mean," the old housekeeper said. "I've been in your shoes once before myself. One of these days, that man is gonna wake up and see his real reason for wanting you near him. Take it from me," Sadie said, reassuringly. "I know my Gabe."

"But you're wrong this time," Joelle insisted.

"Well, we'll just have to see about that, now won't we?" Sadie replied.

Joelle gazed at the old housekeeper. "Now, Sadie, don't you get any wild ideas. Regardless of what you think, Gabriel has a right to his own feelings."

Sadie smiled. "Like I said, don't you worry none. I know what I'm doing."

Joelle turned and gazed longingly out the window toward the cane fields where she knew her husband was hard at work. "I wish I could believe that, Sadie. I really do."

But, of course, she didn't. Gabriel had made his needs for her quite plain and they had nothing to do with love, or happiness, for that matter. And while she might've wished he felt differently toward her and hoped that someday he would, she simply couldn't let herself lose sight of the fact that he didn't right now.

That night, much to her disappointment, Gabriel was so exhausted from his long day of work, he fell asleep within minutes of their going to bed together. This time, Joelle was the one who snuggled closer to him and eventually fell asleep with the security of knowing he was near.

By the time she awoke next morning, Gabriel was already at work, again. But when she went downstairs for breakfast, Sadie was waiting to tell her that he was planning to come back at noon so he could go along with her to her doctor's appointment.

In spite of herself, Joelle was pleased to know he was going with her.

In fact, it had a way of renewing her energy level and she suddenly found herself ready to take on the world. She indulged Sadie by allowing the woman to give her another one of her so-called cooking lessons. Actually she now wanted to learn as much as she could from Sadie. Suddenly it seemed as important to her as reestablishing her career.

Uh-huh. No way, she quickly told herself. Her career was still the most important thing to her. Wasn't it?

Well, of course, it was. Or, at least it would be in time. After her baby was born and she made a triumphant return to the business world. But, for now, it seemed, thinking about the baby had begun to give her all the pleasure and contentment she needed. Surprisingly, lately she found herself enjoying thoughts of being a mother and was now actually looking forward to all the wonderful things she planned to teach her child. Things that only a loving mother could. In fact, it was impossible now for her to try to picture herself without her baby snug in her womb. He—because she was almost certain she was going to have a boy—had somehow become that much a part of her.

In fact, her pregnancy made her think a lot about her own childhood and the problems she had had with her father. She wondered how he was doing, if he was even missing her. She hadn't heard a word from him since she'd left San Diego with Gabriel. Sometimes she thought of calling him. But the truth was, she wasn't the one still angry.

Later that morning, about an hour before noon, Joelle went upstairs, showered and dressed. She tried on several outfits before finding one that still fit her comfortably. It was amazing to her just how much her baby was growing inside her. Especially lately, in the past few weeks. Almost everything she tried on was too tight at her waistline. Not only that, but she was beginning to develop a nice little pouch to her stomach, too—which, as crazy as it seemed, delighted her no end. In fact, standing there in only her skimpy lace bra and panty, she splayed her hands across her lower abdomen and examined herself this way and that in the long mirror hanging on the inside of Gabriel's closet door. And she was right, she thought to herself with a smile. Her stomach was no longer as flat as a pancake. Thinking herself alone in her own little world, she continued to admire and be awed by the changes she saw in her own body.

And that's exactly the way Gabriel found her a few moments later. She didn't hear when he opened the bedroom door. She knew he was there only after he cleared his throat.

She whirled around to face him and saw him standing at a distance with his cap pushed back on his head and a grin as big as Texas on his face.

"Like what you see?" he asked, teasingly.

She startled, almost jumping out of her skin before making a wild dash for something to cover herself with.

She was in no mood to be teased. "Don't you ever knock?"

"Not when I'm opening my own bedroom door," he replied.

By this time Joelle had wrapped herself in a lap blanket she'd found folded on the foot of the bed. Sadie must've laid it there.

His grin slipped up one side of his face. "I liked what you were wearing a moment ago much better."

Joelle sucked up her courage and reminded herself that she had a sense of humor, too. Somewhere. "I was thinking of wearing that outfit to the doctor. What do you think?" she said, cockily, although her knees were shaking.

He gave her a slow once-over. "I think you'll cause quite a stir. Needless to say, you've got me all stirred up."

With pulses racing, Joelle gaped at him. "W-we don't have much time," she stammered, suddenly realizing that their game had just gone too far. "Therefore, if we don't hurry up, we'll be late for my appointment."

He sauntered up to her with that grin of his still on his face, and like a little fool, she stood there and waited for him to reach her. "We won't be late," he drawled, and then his hand came up to the side of her face. Then, suddenly, he took her lips with his.

The nerve of him.

Within moments, the lap blanket she had wrapped around herself fell to the floor. A second later Gabe literally picked her up by the waist and brought her up hard against him.

Her insides melted like butter in a hot oven.

He kissed her passionately, his hands moving over her body and thrilling her beyond description. She was putty in the palms of his hands, and dammit all, he knew it.

Then, all at once, he released her and grinned. "You were so hot in Mexico. I knew you were going to like this new arrangement between us."

Joelle gaped at him momentarily and then clamped her mouth shut. Truthfully she was much too upset with her own memory of that night to deny his accusations. Besides, what was the point in doing so? He knew he was right about her behavior that night, and so did she.

Chapter Nine

Joelle liked her new obstetrician. She was young and enthusiastic and seemed to thoroughly enjoy answering all of her and Gabriel's questions concerning her pregnancy. In fact, her doctor commented that more fathers should be as concerned about their wives as Gabriel. But Joelle wasn't fooled by his interest. She knew it was for the baby, and not her.

Too bad it couldn't have been for both.

In truth, it seemed the entire day belonged to Gabriel. Even their shopping spree later that afternoon turned into quite a fanfare for him. He not only sat there and told her what he liked and didn't like from the variety of maternity styles she modeled, but he did the same for two other women as well who were shopping alone in that area of the store. They both kept telling Joelle how lucky she was to have such a sweet, thoughtful husband.

But then all too soon it was time to go home and once again Gabriel resumed his normal, distant way of interacting with her. Truthfully Joelle couldn't figure out what his problem was. But, whatever it was, it seemed to disappear only when they were in bed together. It was only during the nighttime hours that he gave her the solace she craved from him.

The following days...weeks...passed with very little change, with the exception of Joelle's figure. She was sixteen weeks pregnant now, and because of her slim build, her pregnancy was really beginning to show. On her second visit to her obstetrician, she measured Joelle's stomach and said that the baby's growth pattern was normal. Gabriel had gone along with her for the visit and they were able to listen to their baby's heartbeat. The sound of it wasn't anything like what Joelle was expecting. Or, Gabriel, for that matter. They'd both just stared at each other in awe.

According to Sadie, Joelle was blossoming, and truthfully, Joelle didn't mind the changes taking place with her body. And, if Gabriel's ardent lovemaking at night was any indication of his feelings, he didn't mind, either.

For the most part, Gabriel was still getting up at the crack of dawn and was already hard at work by the time Joelle came downstairs each morning for breakfast. She continued to take her daily lessons in housekeeping from Sadie, but she was beginning to think that she simply wasn't born to be a good housewife. Oh, the cleaning part was okay. It was preparing the meals that was still giving her nightmares. It seemed she was always forgetting to add some main ingredient to a recipe. She either undercooked or overcooked just about everything. One day, she even forgot three eggs boiling on the stove and they were scorched. The smell was awful. It made Joelle sick to her stomach.

But when nighttime came and she and Gabriel retired to bed together, the change that came over them was almost strange. Once the lights were turned off, the stark darkness seemed to give them the courage they needed to set aside their own fears and make love to each other. They could pretend, lie and even ignore their true feelings. They were actors, who were simply being themselves, and yet, they didn't know it.

But, for Joelle, loving Gabriel at night was better than not having the chance to love him at all. It allowed her to continue with the hope that maybe someday he'd come to love her, as well.

She woke up one morning feeling great, dressed in a pair of red stretch pants and an oversize white T-shirt and came rushing downstairs, determined to make the best of the bright sunshiny day. She could smell bacon frying and fresh coffee brewing and knew that Sadie had breakfast waiting for her. She'd been living in Gabriel's house for two months now and knew there was a small throw rug at the foot of the stairs. Undoubtedly she should've been paying closer attention to it, but, unfortunately, on this particular morning, her thoughts were elsewhere. Her foot came down at the middle of the rug and then, suddenly, her foot— the rug—both just slipped out from under her.

She didn't actually fall sitting down. She was able to grab hold of the banister on the staircase and prevent that from happening. However, she did feel when she twisted a muscle in her side. She screamed, and that brought Sadie running to her side within a matter of seconds.

"Oh, child, are you all right?" she asked.

"I slipped," Joelle said, now rubbing a knot that was forming just above her left ear. She'd bumped that side of her head against the wall. Taking a deep breath, she told herself to calm down.

Sadie paled. "I'd better call an ambulance."

"No, Sadie, I'm fine," she said.

"I don't think we should take any chances," Sadie said, frowning down at her. "I'd better send someone for Gabe." With that said, she ran off toward the kitchen. A moment later, she was back.

"One of the hired-hands was raking leaves out back. He's going for Gabe."

"Maybe I should sit down," Joelle said, now feeling a bit shaky. But she felt certain it was only the aftershock of having almost fallen.

Thank goodness, she hadn't.

Sadie helped her to a nearby chair. "I wish Gabe would hurry up," she said, worry etched on her face.

Joelle honestly thought she was okay. She didn't feel bad, or hurt anywhere except for her head and that muscle in her side. And her ankle was aching a little. She'd probably twisted it in her struggle to keep her balance.

But all in all, she was okay. That meant her baby was safe, too.

In fact, thinking of any other possibility just made her want to cry. And she didn't want to cry. Not now. Her baby needed her to be strong.

She heard when the kitchen door flew open, banging against the wall. A moment later, Gabriel came rushing into the room, his face ashen with worry.

"What happened?" he asked, dropping onto one knee in front of Joelle.

"I slipped and almost fell," Joelle said, and in spite of herself, her eyes suddenly filled with tears. Her mouth quivered. "Do you think the baby's all right?"

"I don't know," he said, his features pinched together in a frown. "Yeah, I guess so," he added when he saw her fallen expression.

"I should've removed that stupid throw rug from here a long time ago," Sadie said, unconsciously taking the blame for what had just happened to Joelle.

"It's not your fault," Joelle told her. "I should've been watching my step."

"Call an ambulance, Sadie," Gabriel ordered.

Sadie went to the telephone and dialed 911.

Now the thought of something happening to her baby seemed all too real to Joelle and she began to cry. "I'm sorry," she said, between tears. "I'm so sorry."

"It'll be all right, Joelle. Don't be scared," Gabriel said to her. Then he turned to Sadie. "Ask them if there is anything we should be checking for while the ambulance is on its way. Shouldn't she be lying down?"

A moment later, Sadie replied, "They say not to move her any more than necessary."

Gabriel gazed back at Joelle. "Are you okay?"

Her head throbbed. She was beginning to feel nauseated. "Yes."

Burrowing his eyebrows together, he gently pushed her hair from her face. "Are you sure?"

Joelle felt herself grow weak. "I hit my head."

"Sadie," he yelled back over his shoulder, "get me a cold washcloth."

Sadie was at Gabriel's side in no time at all and handed him a blue washcloth. He began wiping Joelle's face.

"I think she could use an ice pack for this bump on her head," he said, examining her injury.

"I'll get one," Sadie replied.

Joelle felt dizzy. "I think I'm going to be sick," she said.

"That's all right," Gabriel replied, still wiping her face over and over, again. "If you need to, just go ahead and be sick. I'm here. I'll take care of you."

The ambulance arrived soon afterward. Once Joelle was stabilized, she was brought to the hospital. Gabriel and Sadie followed the ambulance in his truck.

Her obstetrician was called in and she immediately ordered an ultrasound. Studying the images on the monitor, she determined that Joelle's baby had apparently suffered no ill effects from her fall. However, Joelle herself did have a slight concussion from the blow to the side of her head, and she was undoubtedly going to have some sore muscles to contend with. She was ordered to stay in bed a few days and, then just to be on the safe side, was told to limit her physical activities for the next couple of weeks, including intercourse. Neither Joelle nor Gabriel commented on that one. The only proof Joelle had that he'd heard the instructions her doctor was giving her was when his eyes lifted up and met hers briefly. Gabriel assured her doctor that he would see to it that she carefully followed all instructions for her recovery. After eight long hours in the hospital, Joelle was finally released and allowed to go home.

Once they arrived back at the plantation, Gabriel didn't even let her climb the stairs up to their bedroom. After insisting that Sadie get some rest, he carried Joelle to bed, and helped her to get into a nightgown as if it was something he did every night. Truthfully he had more experience in doing just the opposite. Then, after tucking her in and giving her instructions to stay in bed, he kissed her lightly on the forehead and went back downstairs to fix her something to eat. He came back up with a bed tray full of food.

Gabriel assisted in trying to get her comfortably propped up on several pillows. Afterward, he set the tray over her lap, pulled a chair up alongside her bed and sat down. That's when Joelle noticed that there were two bowls of potato soup on the tray.

"I didn't see the point in my going back downstairs to eat alone in the kitchen while you ate up here by yourself."

"I agree," she said, liking the idea that they were going to share this time together. Truthfully, here lately, she could've spent her every waking moment with him, and still it wouldn't have been enough to fill the void in her; the void caused, by knowing she would always have his commitment to their marriage, but never his love.

Gabriel glanced at the old firebox in his bedroom. "I haven't used the fireplace up here in years. But, I was thinking, since you're going to have to stay in bed for a few days, it might be kind of nice if I cleaned it out so we could use it."

Joelle knew she was being foolish for taking this simple thoughtfulness from him so deep into her heart. He was just being nice, after all, to the woman who was going to have his baby.

"Thank you," she said. "That's very thoughtful of you."

He grinned. "I'd get you a portable TV, too, but then you'd probably sleep all the time."

She smiled. "You're probably right."

Suddenly, unable to contain herself a moment longer, she reached out and touched his arm. "Gabriel," she said, "I'm really sorry about today. I know I must have worried you, considering what could've happened to the baby and all."

He glanced down to where her fingers held him. "Yeah," he said, gruffly. "I was scared to death when I was told that you'd fallen. I thought the worst had happened."

"Yes," she said, knowing he meant her losing the baby, "me, too." Then, suddenly realizing that she was still holding on to his arm, she released him and blushed.

He finished his bowl of soup and set it down on the tray. Leaning back in his chair, he watched her take several bites of her food before saying, "How are the cooking lessons with Sadie going?"

In fact, she'd had no idea that he was still aware she was taking them. He always seemed so preoccupied with other matters, she hadn't thought he'd been paying attention to what she had been doing during the day.

"Terrible," she said, deciding that it wasn't going to do her any good to lie. After all, the proof was in the pudding, and let's face it, in her case, it was usually tasteless. She shrugged. "I guess I'm not cut out to be domesticated, after all."

He smiled as if he wasn't at all surprised by her reply. "Well, there's always your career."

Joelle smirked. "Yeah, there's always that," she said, dryly.

For whatever reason, that seemed to be the end of their meal and their conversation, both at the same time. Gabriel carried the tray of empty bowls downstairs, then came back up and showered. By the time he climbed into bed next to Joelle, she had slipped down under the covers and was anxious for him to be next to her.

"Good night," he said, turning off the bedside lamp.

"Good night," she replied.

"Are you cold?"

"A little," she said.

"Me, too," Gabriel replied, and then he scooted over to her side of the bed. "Come here. I'll hold you awhile."

Joelle didn't argue with him. He opened his arms and she slipped right into them.

He was naked, as always.

And hard.

Her stomach quivered.

But her doctor had said . . .

"Is that better?" he asked, his tone of voice having grown hoarse.

"Mmm . . . much," she replied.

"Then sleep tight, Ames."

"You, too, Lafleur."

And for the next couple of weeks, that was how they went to bed each night. With Gabriel sliding across to her side and Joelle coming willingly into his arms. It was killing her to be so close to him, and yet so far away. But, it was better than nothing, and besides, she didn't have to worry about being cold at night. His strong, hard body pressed against hers kept her all snug and warm.

And hot.

But that was beside the point.

They couldn't be intimate right now, and that's all there was to it.

The following days rolled by quickly. Joelle's baby was gaining weight—and so was she. Sadie said she was radiant, and sometimes, on a really good day, she actually felt that way. Pregnancy wasn't turning out to be so bad, after all. Just like everything else in life, it was a learning experience. And, if nothing else, she was a good learner, except, of course, when it came to cooking. Sadie, Joelle thought, had finally given up on her.

The weather in south Louisiana was getting warmer now and Gabriel's fields were almost all planted. His days were still long, however, and she seldom saw him during the daylight hours.

The first time she felt her baby kick was completely unexpected. It happened one night at the supper table when she, Gabriel and Sadie were all seated. Dropping her fork, she gasped in surprise. Her hands automatically went to her stomach.

"What's wrong?" Gabriel asked, his eyes widening.

Joelle laughed deep in her throat. "It was the baby," she exclaimed, excitedly, her own eyes widening. "He just kicked me."

Gabriel's face went blank. "He kicked you?"

"Yes," Joelle said, giggling. "He kicked me."

"You're kidding."

"No. Oh…!" she said a moment later. "He just did it again."

Spellbound, Gabriel rose and pushed back his chair. Within a fraction of a second, he was at her side. Without thinking, Joelle grabbed his hand and placed it palm down on her stomach. The room fell silent and they waited for even the slightest motion from within.

A couple of seconds ticked by. And, then, *wham!* He kicked her again.

"There," she said, "did you feel it?" she asked, excitedly, gazing at her husband's face.

Gabriel looked awed. "I felt it," he said. Then he knelt down and placed his ear against her stomach and listened. After a moment, he said, "Sadie, come here. You can feel my baby moving."

His baby. Whoa. What had happened to *their* baby? Joelle wondered. Or, even, the baby. Why did he have to make it sound as if it was just his baby and that she didn't account for any part of it? She should've been more important to him than that. Truthfully she'd deserved better.

But the fact of the matter was, she didn't feel of any importance to him. Only in the context that she was carrying his child, therefore he had to be concerned about her welfare. He desired her, but that didn't mean anything, either. Certainly it didn't mean what she needed it to, and sooner or later she was going to have to accept that fact and quit hoping for something that simply wasn't going to happen.

Still and all, in spite of herself, after Gabriel fell asleep that night, she let her emotions get the better of her and quietly cried herself to sleep.

Winter disappeared and spring crept over the land. The days grew warmer and once again Louisiana became a state of narrow bayous and lush greenery. Azaleas bloomed, and then finally the pecan trees budded new leaves. According to Gabriel, that alone was a promise that spring was finally here.

As soon as her doctor gave Joelle an approval of good health, she and Gabriel resumed their lovemaking each night. But he was always gentle and caring of the fact that she was pregnant with his child, and maybe it was because of his gentleness that Joelle continued to look forward to their intimacies.

One morning Joelle woke up and realized that she'd dreamed of her father. Deciding to be the one to put her pride aside first, she called him, but was soon disappointed to find out that he was away on a business trip abroad. She left a message for him to call her back, but he never did. The fact that he could so easily dismiss her from his life only added to her heartache. Actually Sadie was the only person in her life right now that seemed to care about her. If it hadn't been for Sadie, Joelle felt sure her loneliness would've been intolerable.

But these days, even Sadie was busy with other matters. Her only sister, who lived in Birmingham, Alabama, was in the area for a few days and they were spending a lot of time together. In fact, Sadie informed Joelle that she and her sister were going out for dinner that night, therefore, it was going to be up to her to put the homemade potpie into the oven for supper. Joelle had given up trying to learn to be a cook, but she assured Sadie that she would place her potpie into the oven and bake it to perfection. After bustling around and giving Joelle a slew of instructions to follow, Sadie finally left with her sister.

At exactly five-thirty that afternoon, Joelle turned on the oven to the temperature Sadie had suggested and then a few minutes later, slipped the potpie inside. Afterward she went upstairs, took a bath and came back down feeling refreshed. It took her only about thirty-five minutes. The potpie still had ten more minutes to bake.

Looking for something to do to keep her busy for those few minutes, Joelle padded around the house, first in the kitchen and then by thoughtlessly walking into Gabriel's study. She didn't notice when she bumped the door stop on her way in. She realized it when the door closed on its own behind her a couple of seconds later. Turning to leave the room, she was walking out when her gaze fell on some photos stacked together on a shelf.

Joelle didn't consider herself being nosy when she picked up the snapshots and began to look through them. They were, after all, photographs that Gabriel had taken while he was on vacation in Acupulco. They must have been the ones that Sadie had mentioned once because Joelle recognized herself in many of them. Truthfully she was amazed to see that Gabriel had taken so many of her. Sitting on the edge of the sofa, she studied one snapshot after the other.

Minutes passed. To Joelle, it seemed to be only a few. Suddenly she heard a loud noise and then Gabriel's panicked voice shouting her name. Startled, Joelle jumped to her feet, dropping the snapshot on the floor, and raced for the door. Opening it, she stood there in shock. The kitchen was filled with smoke.

My God, the house was on fire, and she'd been sitting in his study, completely unaware.

Suddenly Gabriel was at her side and was lifting her into his arms. Within moments, he had them outside on the porch.

"What's happening?" she asked.

"The house," he said, gasping for breath, and Joelle realized that he must have been searching the smoke-filled house for her. "Is on fire," he finally said.

"I didn't even know..." Joelle's voice trailed off as a sudden thought took center stage in her mind. "Oh, no!" Joelle exclaimed, lifting her hands to her cheeks. "I forgot the pie in the oven."

She heard Gabriel curse loudly. Standing her on her feet, he immediately barreled back into the house. It all happened so fast, Joelle just stood there in shock. Within seconds, he came back out again, only this time he was carrying what was left of Sadie's chicken potpie. The pie crust was charred and smoking. Gabriel threw it on the ground and glared at her. "What in the hell were you thinking about?"

"I—I don't know," Joelle replied, dazed by what all was happening.

"You damned near burned my house down," he exclaimed, and his features were hardened with anger.

Joelle's knees were weak from shock. "I'm sorry," she stammered. "I . . . I'm so sorry."

He placed his hands on his hips. "What in the hell were you doing while the house was filling up with smoke?"

"I—uh—nothing, really," she stammered. She felt like such an idiot. Like the worthless person her father thought she was.

"Do you have any idea how long it's going to take us to get that smell out of the house?"

And then suddenly something inside her decided that she wasn't that worthless person, after all. True, she wasn't perfect, either. She'd simply made a mistake, dammit. In fact, it took a strong person to admit a mistake.

And while his precious house might've been smoky, not one solitary inch of it—other than the pie, that was—was burned.

"Look, Gabriel, I made a mistake. I'm truly sorry. I know it was thoughtless of me to forget about the pie, but—"

"Just make damned sure you don't make that kind of mistake, again."

She glanced up and saw that he was still glaring at her.

"In fact," he said, "from now on, stay out of the kitchen and just let Sadie do all the cooking."

Hurt, the only thing Joelle could do was gaze at him. In that moment it seemed to her that the only way she was of any real use to him was as a bed warmer. Well, a forty-nine dollar electric blanket from a discount outlet could do that.

She was fighting back tears. Tears that she refused to let him see. "I hate it here," she said, a part of her wishing she could hurt him as much as he was hurting her.

He smirked. "Well, don't feel so bad. Because there's not a day that goes by that I don't regret bringing you here."

"You bastard," she said, and then she stormed off.

It wasn't until nine o'clock that night before Gabriel finished cleaning up the house, airing out the rooms and discarding what was too smoke-saturated to be of any more use. The entire time, Joelle sat on the front porch with the mosquitoes and the calm quietness of night. She had lied when she'd said she hated it here. In truth, she'd come to love this old plantation as if it was her own. But it wasn't hers, and it never would be.

Sadie returned home just in time to help Gabriel close up the house. She tried soothing Joelle's hurt feelings, but in truth, no one other than Gabriel could've done that. But he wasn't even trying. When it came time to go to bed that night, he slept in the extra bedroom that Joelle had used when she'd first arrived.

Which was perfectly fine with her.

Early the next morning, Joelle woke up to find Gabriel standing at the foot of her bed. Lifting herself up on her elbows, she gazed at him in question.

"Look," he said, apologetically, "I'm sorry about yesterday. I acted like a jerk."

"Fine," she replied dryly.

"I mean it."

"Okay. I accept your apology."

Gabriel gazed at her for a couple of moments, then finally nodded and walked away.

Joelle lay back down and this time tears did fill her eyes. Yes, he was probably sorry for what he'd said out loud to her, but that didn't change the fact that he'd meant what he'd said.

Which should've come as no big surprise to her, considering she'd known all along that was how he felt. Still, it did have an effect on her, and she was beginning to doubt if she could continue much longer with the deal they'd made concerning the baby. How could she live with a man who really didn't want her around?

Two days passed. They were polite to each other and on the second night Gabriel returned to his bed to sleep with her. But that was all they did.

The following morning, Sadie answered the telephone and then handed the receiver to Joelle, saying it was long distance. Immediately, Joelle's heart leaped into her throat. She thought it was her father, calling her at last.

But it wasn't her father. It was his secretary, instead, and the news she had to give Joelle concerning her father was grim. Sylvan Ames had suffered a massive stroke during the night and was in intensive care at a hospital in San Diego. He was asking for Joelle.

Stunned, Joelle assured the woman that she would be on the next flight home. Then, after explaining to Sadie what had happened, she called the airport and made reservations on a flight leaving the New Orleans airport in less than four hours. With little time to spare, she went upstairs and began packing for her trip. Sadie followed at her heels.

"Oh, my Lord. I wonder what Gabe is gonna have to say about you having to leave so suddenly."

Joelle didn't bother to answer. Right now she felt she had other things to worry about. Actually Gabriel had proven that he was quite capable of taking care of himself in any crisis. Whatever minor effect her leaving would have on him, it would be temporary. Of that much she was certain.

Sadie carefully folded the clothes Joelle tossed on the bed to take with her. "Maybe," she said, thoughtfully, "I ought to go out to the field and tell him what's happened."

"There's no need for that," Joelle said. "I plan to call a cab to drive me to the airport."

"But maybe I should go tell him, anyway," Sadie replied. A moment later, without telling Joelle where she was going, she left the bedroom and went downstairs. Joelle was so preoccupied with her own thoughts, she didn't even notice.

She had only one thing on her mind. For the first time in her life, her father needed her.

She finished packing one suitcase and closed it. Then, turning to go back to the closet for additional clothes, she saw Gabriel enter the room.

Frowning, he shoved his cap back on his head and then placed his hands on his hips. "What are you doing?" he asked.

"Packing," she replied, steadily, but her heart was actually pounding like crazy. "My father's had a stroke and I've got to get to him as soon as possible."

Gabriel's frown deepened. "Just like that," he said, suddenly walking toward her. "Without even bothering to let me know first."

Joelle shrugged. "I knew Sadie would tell you."

"But not you," he said, his tone of voice having a definite edge to it.

"No," she replied, without looking at him. "Not me." She continued to add items to the one suitcase she had left to pack. "Frankly I didn't think it would matter to you, one way or the other."

"It matters," he growled. "You're my wife."

Slamming shut her second suitcase, Joelle pulled it from the bed and sat it on the floor. "That," she replied, coolly, this time lifting her gaze to his, "is debatable." However, a lump the size of a golf ball settled in her throat.

"We have a deal," he said.

"I know that," Joelle replied.

"Well, are you going to continue to honor it, or what?"

Joelle turned and faced Gabriel. "Look, right now all I can think about is my father lying in a hospital in critical condition, asking for me."

Gabriel's hands came back to his hips and he glanced away in obvious frustration. "Yeah, you're right," he said.

She walked past him and he grabbed her by the arm. She glanced up at him.

"When do you leave?" he asked.

"A taxi is on its way to pick me up now."

"I see," he said. Then lifting her two suitcases, he added, "In that case, I'll carry these downstairs for you."

"Thank you," she replied.

Gabriel nodded and then walked out of the room with them.

And by the time Joelle came downstairs, Sadie told her that he'd already gone back to work in the fields. "Gabe ain't much on partings," she said, shaking her head sadly. "Not even when it's only temporary. He told me to tell you goodbye."

With a weak smile on her lips, Joelle nodded. "Tell him I said the same."

And by the time the taxi arrived to pick her up for the two-hour drive to the airport, there was little doubt in Joelle's mind that she was never coming back.

And so when she said her final goodbye to Sadie, she found her heart was already breaking into a million tiny pieces.

Chapter Ten

Oddly enough, San Diego now seemed completely foreign to Joelle. Almost as if it had been years since she'd lived there, instead of just a few months. It was painfully clear that she no longer belonged to the city she had grown up in. Suddenly it was too noisy—and too busy—and much too crowded for her liking. She missed the country...the quiet...the darkness. She missed Sadie...her cooking...and her wisdom. But most of all she missed Gabriel and the love she had wanted so desperately for him to give her. Even now a part of her longed to be in his arms just once more, but that was never to be. She knew that Gabriel was expecting her to return to him, but she didn't think she could. Not without losing an important part of herself in the process. And, surprisingly, it had nothing to do with her having or not having a career. It had to do with who she was inside. And she deserved better than a marriage without love.

If only she'd gotten a letter or a telephone call from him in the past days, maybe it would've helped. Somehow, she would've found a way to forgive his cruel words from that night when she'd forgotten the potpie in the oven. But she'd been in California almost three weeks now, and the only person she'd heard from during that time was Sadie, who called every few days to see how she, the baby and her father were all doing. But she never once mentioned Gabriel's name to Joelle. Joelle knew without a doubt that Sadie was sharing the news she received with him. In fact, for all she knew, Gabriel was the one telling her to place the calls. But it wasn't the same as talking to him. It was growing plainer by the day that, in spite of his need for an heir, he was glad that *she* was out of his life for the time being. Once when Sadie called, Joelle had thought she'd heard his voice in the background. But she wasn't sure, and she hadn't asked. Eventually, she'd shoved that thought aside. After all, Sadie had placed that particular phone call in the middle of the afternoon, a time when Gabriel normally would've been out working in the fields. Therefore, it was highly unlikely that he was home at the time.

Undoubtedly she had just wanted to think it was his voice she'd heard.

For the most part, her father was recuperating as well as could be expected, although a complete recovery was going to take several months of intense rehabilitation. On the positive side, his speech had improved greatly in the past couple of days, and his doctors were saying that he might be able to go home within the week.

On the night before her father was to be released from the hospital, Joelle stayed with him later than usual and arrived home around eight-thirty. When she unlocked the door, the telephone was ringing. Not sure of exactly who she was expecting, she rushed to pick it up before her father's butler could. "Hello," she said, anxiously.

"Joelle," Gabriel said a moment later, "it's me. Gabe."

"Oh," she said, relieved, and yet every cell in her body went on alert. She breathed in deeply. Each time the phone had rung over the past few weeks, she'd hoped it was Gabriel's voice she'd hear when she picked up the receiver. Now that it was, she couldn't think of one single thing to say.

"How's your father?" he asked. "Sadie's been keeping me informed of his recovery. I understand that he's getting out of the hospital soon."

"Tomorrow," she replied, trying desperately to clear the lump in her throat.

"That's good," he replied, and in some ways he sounded almost as ill at ease as she felt. "And how are you and the baby doing?"

"Fine."

"Great," he replied. "I—uh..." He cleared his throat. "I was just browsing through the snapshots I took of you in Acapulco," he said.

"Oh?" she said.

"Well, I mean, I was looking at all the snapshots and several of them are of you," he answered.

"I see," she replied, recalling her own memories of them. But what was his point, anyway?

Gabriel cleared his throat. "I—uh—well, I was thinking that maybe you might want to show them to your father. I could send them to you."

"The snapshots?" she inquired.

"Yeah—well, it was just a thought, but maybe not such a good one, after all," he replied.

A long, dead silence followed.

Eventually Gabriel cleared his throat. "Uh...look, Joelle, I was wondering if you had any idea when you'd be coming back home."

Home. How she longed to be home. If only he truly wanted her there. Her and the baby, and not just the baby.

With a heaviness at the center of her chest, Joelle paused. "I don't know. I simply don't know if I can go back to you, Gabriel."

"What do you mean, *if you can?* Of course, you can. I can come and get you whenever you want. Just say the word."

"But that's just it, Gabriel," Joelle said, sadly. "I don't know if I want to go back."

There was another long pause. Finally he said, "We have a deal, Joelle."

"I know."

"Do you realize what this is going to mean?"

"Yes. It means that you and I will have to share custody of our child."

"Exactly. And that's good enough for you?"

Joelle sighed deeply. "It may end up being the best I can offer," she replied, once again fighting back those tears she hated to have anyone see.

"You're making a mistake, Ames."

"Well, it certainly won't be my first, now will it?" she said, and from the quietness that followed, she knew he was remembering one of her last mistakes. The night he'd accused her of almost burning down his house.

"I said I was sorry about that," he replied.

"And I said I accepted your apology," she said pointedly.

Gabriel sighed heavily in the telephone. Then a moment later he seemed to grow almost angry as he said, "You'd better think about this, Joelle, before you take any action to end our marriage."

"Which one?" she replied dryly. Considering the tension she was under, she was quite proud of herself for being able to think so quickly.

She obviously stunned him, because he didn't reply for the longest time. Finally he said, "Either one."

A moment later, he added, "I'll be in touch." And then he hung up.

Releasing a deeply held sigh, Joelle turned and headed up the stairs. Her heart was aching so badly, she couldn't help herself. When she reached the privacy of her bedroom, she began to cry.

Rubbing the back of his neck in the hopes of relieving some of the tension, Gabriel went outside and strolled in the darkness surrounding his house.

Damn her, anyway. She really had some nerve to decide now that she didn't want to hold up her end of their bargain. Just who did she think she was, anyway? She couldn't do this to him and get away with it. As the father of her baby, he had his rights.

He sighed heavily. Ah, to hell with rights and all that stuff. That wasn't even the issue, anymore. Frankly, as far as he was concerned, *she* was the issue. She'd come into his home, worked her way into his heart and now she wanted out.

Dammit, it wasn't fair.

Not when they were going to have a child together.

Not when he'd made love to her more times than he could remember. Didn't that count for something?

Apparently, to her, it didn't.

What more did she want from him? She'd had his commitment to their marriage—and now, in spite of his struggle to the contrary, she had his heart, too. He'd tried everything to keep her away from his soul. He'd even told her he didn't want her here with him, when, actually, just the opposite was true. She was driving him crazy, and in truth, it had nothing to do with the baby she was carrying. It had to do with her. She'd grabbed hold of him the first time he'd seen her that day in Mexico and she hadn't let go of him yet.

And now he no longer wanted her to let go. In fact, he wanted to build a life together. It was what he wanted more than anything in the world.

He was sure she wanted that, too. But, until now, he had been holding back his feelings, leaving her uncertain of how he felt about her. That all had to change.

He'd been a real jerk, all right, in the hopes of protecting his heart. He owed Joelle a deep, heartfelt apology. Suddenly the words to a song he'd once heard came to mind. *Climb the highest mountain. Swim the deepest sea.*

Yeah, he was ready to do those things, and more if necessary, to make her believe him. She was his world.

She and their baby. And this was their home. One way or the other, he had to make her see that.

The following morning, Gabriel came down to breakfast with a new spring to his step and announced to Sadie that he was leaving for California later that day. Without a moment's hesitation, Sadie said, "Well, it took you long enough to come to your senses. I'll have your suitcase packed in no time at all."

And then, as she went about her chores, she began to hum a lively little French tune that she always did when she was happy.

Gabe smiled. "I knew I could count on you, Sadie." Then he kissed her on the cheek. "Thanks for everything."

She smiled and then swatted him playfully. "Now, git on out of here. You got work to do before you can leave."

He laughed and quickly scooted out the door, whistling that same little tune his housekeeper was humming.

It was late afternoon when Gabriel arrived in San Diego. He took a cab to Joelle's father's address, which turned out to be located in a very secluded part of San Diego. Without a hint of intimidation, he got out, rang the doorbell and waited. The butler finally came to the door.

"I'm here to see my wife," Gabriel announced.

The butler eyeballed him intently, from the tips of his athletic shoes to the top of his baseball cap. "Then you must be Mr. Lafleur."

"That's right," Gabriel replied.

The butler cleared his throat. "Then I'll get Ms....Joelle," he countered.

"I'd appreciate that," Gabriel said.

The butler motioned for him to step inside, so he did. The man went to an intercom, pushed a button and then announced that Gabe was here. The answer that came back was too low for Gabriel to hear, but he thought it sounded like Joelle's voice. His heart raced ahead.

"She'll be right down," the butler said, implying that she was upstairs. Gabe automatically turned and began watching for her to descend the staircase. He was so anxious to see her, his guts were all in knots.

Finally she came into view and his heart really began to pound with each step she took toward him.

She looked beautiful, like a dream come true, and his eyes ate up the sight of her. Looking up, he walked to the foot of the stairs and waited for her to reach him.

"Hello, Gabriel," she said.

"Hello, Joelle."

"Why are you here?" she asked, point-blank, hesitating as she came down the last step.

He smiled tentatively. "I was hoping that would be pretty obvious to you."

She shrugged. "It is," she replied. "I know how much this baby means to you."

"That it does," he replied with a sheepish grin. "But it isn't the only thing that means the world to me. It has just taken me a while to realize that."

Joelle's heart slammed against her chest, in spite of the fact she'd warned herself against such foolishness before coming down to greet him. No matter what, she'd promised herself not to react to anything he said.

He didn't love her, and that was that. She was back in her world. She had her father's support now. She could deal with it.

"Look," he said, breathlessly. "I'm going to get right to the point. I've been a jerk, a fool, an idiot, and I know I don't deserve your forgiveness. If you told me to get out of here right now and never come back, I'd understand."

Oh, that doggone heart of hers, Joelle thought to herself. It was beating out of control, regardless of her warnings to the contrary. It was just that she loved him so much and always would. "What are you trying to say?" she asked, breathlessly, trying desperately to keep herself calm. She wrapped her arms around herself tightly.

"Dammit, Joelle," he said, grabbing her by the shoulders. "I'm trying to say I love you. I don't know when it happened. Or, how it happened. But, it did and now you're as important to my happiness as anything, or anyone else. And I don't want to live my life without you."

Joelle gaped at him. "Sadie put you up to this," she said.

"No," he said, shaking his head. "It wasn't Sadie, and it isn't the baby. You're the reason I'm here, plain and simple. I need you with me."

Joelle was speechless.

"In fact," he said, grinning at her, "this baby is just the start of things to come. I want us to have a lot more babies. Five, maybe."

"Five?" she exclaimed, her heart swelling with joy.

"Well," he said, with a slight shrug and a grin as bright as the morning sunshine on a clear day, "maybe not five."

Joelle tilted her head in thought. "Well, no doubt Sadie would be thrilled to have five grandchildren," she replied.

Tears glistened in Gabriel's eyes. "What exactly are you saying, Joelle? Do I have your forgiveness?"

Seeing his tears brought moisture to her own eyes. "I'm saying, now that I think about it, five babies sound just about right for us."

"Oh, yeah," he said, his grin now slipping up one side of his handsome face. He tightened his hold on her. "I love you, Joelle."

Joelle wet her lips. "I love you, too," she said. "I have for a long time, now."

Something soared to life in his eyes. "You drive me crazy when you do that," he drawled.

"Do what?" she asked, innocently.

"This," he said, and then he ran the tip of his tongue over her lips.

Every flow of blood in her body did a U-turn and headed for her lower abdomen.

"Oh, that," she replied, returning the favor across his lips.

He kissed her tenderly, and then said, "How's your father doing?"

"He's doing quite well, actually."

"Do you think there will ever come a time when he'll be ready to accept our marriage—our love for each other?"

Joelle smiled. "I think so. He's a changed man since his stroke. My happiness seems to be very important to him."

Gabriel looked deep into her eyes. "I'm glad about that."

"Me, too," she replied.

Gabriel smiled at her. "And to think this all started because of a little too much tequila and a wild idea that we needed to be married."

She smiled back. "Well, at least the idea proved to be a good one."

"The sex that night wasn't so bad, either," he said with a twinkle in his eyes.

And then her husband took her into his arms and kissed her passionately on the mouth.

And that was when Joelle suddenly realized that her one true goal in life had been fulfilled. All her life she had wanted to be accepted and loved for who she was, shortcomings and all. In order to achieve it, she'd strived to be the best in what she thought was important.

And in Gabriel's arms, that's how she felt... loved ... accepted ... fulfilled ... important.   And, sometimes, even perfect.

It was a feeling she would cherish in her heart for all time.

She had strived for perfection, and she had found it at last in Gabriel's love.

Epilogue

Gabriel walked into Joelle's room at the hospital and kissed her on the lips. Their newborn son was sound asleep in the crib right next to her bed.

"How's my little hot tamale," he said, a nickname he'd given her in the past months. He only used it when they were alone. It was in reference, of course, to their first night together in Acapulco. A night neither of them would ever forget. Nor did they want to.

Then he smiled and brought a gift-wrapped package into view. "This is for you," he said, lightly. "I wanted to give you something special and, well...this is what I came up with."

Joelle smiled.

He planted a kiss on her mouth. "Go ahead," he said, anxiously, "open it."

"Okay," she said, thinking of how much she adored her husband. She tore the colorful wrapping from the package and saw it was a picture frame of some kind. A moment later she gasped when she realized that it was the piece of paper that he'd found in his shirt pocket that morning at the hotel in Acapulco. She'd only gotten a glimpse of it back then, but, still, she remembered it all too well. It read, *Gabriel and Joelle, I now pronounce you man and wife. Signed, José Cuervo.*

"It's our original marriage certificate," he said, his eyes twinkling with pleasure. "Remember it?"

Her eyes widened. "Yes, of course... B-but, I remember, you threw it away in the trash can in my hotel room."

Gabriel grinned sheepishly. "I know," he said. "But once you left, I took it out and saved it."

Joelle gaped at him. "But, why?" she asked.

Gabriel shrugged. "To tell you the truth, I don't know. I guess deep down inside I knew even then that we were meant for each other. I know one thing for sure, you're now a valuable part of my life that I can't live without."

Tears sprang into Joelle's eyes. "You're so wonderful to me."

"I'll never be able to do enough to show how much I love you. Never. But I'll never stop trying."

"Don't you dare," Joelle said, playfully punching him in the stomach.

And then Gabriel kissed her again. "I love you, Ames."

"I love you, too, Lafleur," she replied.

"Oh, by the way. Your father called the house today," Gabriel told her. "He says he's doing well and is planning to come for his first grandchild's christening. I told him he was welcome to stay with us for as long as he liked."

Joelle smiled.

Truly, this was turning out to be one of the happiest days of her life.

"Are you ready to go home?" Gabriel asked a moment later. "Sadie's waiting to spoil her first grandchild."

Joelle thought about her father coming to visit them and about Sadie's sometimes—oftentimes—salty opinions on life, and her smile widened. Both her father and Sadie were going to be in for the shock of their lives.

Joelle glanced up and her eyes met Gabriel's. She widened her smile. "I'm ready, my love," she said.

He picked up their son and placed him in her waiting arms. The newborn snuggled his face against the softness of her breast. "He's getting hungry," she said.

"Then let's go home," Gabriel replied, his deep, rich voice vibrating in her ears. And then his arm went around Joelle's shoulders protectively.

And, as always these days, he made Joelle feel as though she were being lifted and carried home on a pedestal.

His love was, indeed, a pedestal.

And it was the perfect resting place for her in the years to come.

It was, in fact, the throne he carried her upon from that day forward.

* * * * * *

Silhouette®

AVAILABLE THIS MONTH FROM SILHOUETTE ROMANCE®

Take 4 bestselling love stories FREE

Plus get a FREE surprise gift!

Bundles of Joy

The biggest romantic surprises come in the smallest packages!

January:

HAVING GABRIEL'S BABY by Kristin Morgan (#1199)

After one night of passion Joelle was expecting! The dad-to-be, rancher Gabriel Lafleur, insisted on marriage. But could they find true love as a family?

April:

YOUR BABY OR MINE? by Marie Ferrarella (#1216)

Single daddy Alec Beckett needed help with his infant daughter! When the lovely Marissa Rogers took the job with an infant of her own, Alec realized he wanted this mom-for-hire *permanently*—as part of a real family!

Don't miss these irresistible Bundles of Joy, coming to you in January and April, only from

❤ Silhouette ROMANCE™

Look us up on-line at: http://www.romance.net

BOJ-J-A

He's able to change a diaper in three seconds flat.
And melt an unsuspecting heart even more quickly.
But changing his mind about marriage might take some doing!
He's more than a man...
He's a **FABULOUS FATHER!**

***

January:
MAD FOR THE DAD by Terry Essig (#1198)
Daniel Van Scott asked Rachel Gatlin for advice on raising his nephew—
and soon noticed her charms as both a mother...*and* a woman.

February:
DADDY BY DECISION by Lindsay Longford (#1204)
Rancher Jonas Riley proposed marriage to Jessica McDonald! But
would Jonas still want her when he found out a secret about her
little boy?

March:
MYSTERY MAN by Diana Palmer (#1210)
50th Fabulous Father! Tycoon Canton Rourke was a man of mystery,
but could the beautiful Janine Curtis find his answers with a lifetime
of love?

May:
MY BABY, YOUR SON by Anne Peters (#1222)
Beautiful April Bingham was determined to reclaim her long-lost child.
Could she also rekindle the love of the boy's father?

***

Celebrate fatherhood—and love!—every month.
FABULOUS FATHERS...only in ▼ *Silhouette* ROMANCE™

Look us up on-line at: http://www.romance.net   FF-J-M

Five irresistible men say "I do" for a lifetime of love
in these lovable novels—our Valentine to you in February!

I'M YOUR GROOM

#1205 *It's Raining Grooms* by Carolyn Zane
After praying every night for a husband, Prudence was suddenly
engaged—to the last man she'd ever expect to marry!

#1206 *To Wed Again?* by DeAnna Talcott
Once Mr. and Mrs., Meredith and Rowe Worth were now adoptive
parents to a little girl. And blessed with a second chance at marriage!

#1207 *An Accidental Marriage* by Judith Janeway
Best man Ryan Holt never wanted to be a groom himself—until a
cover-up left everyone thinking he was married to maid of honor
Kit Kendrick!

#1208 *Husband Next Door* by Anne Ha
When Shelly got engaged to a stable, *boring* fiancé, her neighbor and
very confirmed bachelor Aaron Carpenter suddenly realized *he* was
meant to be her husband!

#1209 *Wedding Rings and Baby Things* by Teresa Southwick
To avoid scandal, very pregnant Kelly Walker needed a husband fast,
not forever. But after becoming Mrs. Mike Cameron, Kelly fell for this
father figure!

Don't miss these five wonderful books,
Available in February 1997,
only from

▼ *Silhouette* ROMANCE™

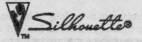

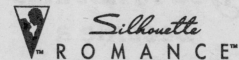

COMING NEXT MONTH

#1204 DADDY BY DECISION—Lindsay Longford
Fabulous Fathers
Charming and sexy Jonas Riley had slipped past Jessica McDonald's defenses years ago. Now the rancher was back—and proposing marriage to the single mom. But would Jonas still want Jessica when he found out the secret about her little boy?

#1205 IT'S RAINING GROOMS—Carolyn Zane
I'm Your Groom
Prudence was praying for a husband when rugged Trent Tanner literally fell from above—through her ceiling! Though Trent was no answered prayer, his request that she pose as his fiancée just might be the miracle Prudence was looking for!

#1206 TO WED AGAIN?—DeAnna Talcott
I'm Your Groom
Once Mr. and Mrs., Meredith and Rowe Worth suddenly found themselves adoptive parents to an adorable little girl. Now that they were learning to bandage boo-boos and read bedtime stories, could they also learn to fall in love and wed—again?

#1207 AN ACCIDENTAL MARRIAGE—Judith Janeway
I'm Your Groom
Best man Ryan Holt had never wanted to become a groom himself—until a last-minute cover-up left everyone thinking he was married to maid of honor Kit Kendrick! Now this confirmed bachelor was captivated by lovely Kit and wished their "marriage" was no accident!

#1208 HUSBAND NEXT DOOR—Anne Ha
I'm Your Groom
When Shelly got engaged to a nice, stable, *boring* fiancé, Aaron Carpenter suddenly realized he was in love with his beautiful neighbor, and set out to convince her that he was her perfect husband—next door!

#1209 WEDDING RINGS AND BABY THINGS—Teresa Southwick
I'm Your Groom
To avoid scandal, single mom-to-be Kelly Walker needed a husband fast, not forever. But after becoming Mrs. Mike Cameron, Kelly was soon falling for this handsome father figure, and hoping for a family for always.